MW00398624

Is the
Cat Lady
Crazy?

Also By Beverly Hurwitz MD

A Walker's Guide to Park City

Park City Hiking Guide

Nobody Else's Business - A Novel

Is the Cat Lady Crazy?

Beverly Hurwitz MD

This story is based on an actual medical case.
All of the people and places in this story are fictional.
Any resemblance to real people or institutions is purely coincidental.

Surrogate Press®

Published in the United States by
Surrogate Press®
an imprint of Faceted Press®
Surrogate Press, LLC
Park City, Utah

SurrogatePress.com

ISBN: 978-1-947459-41-0

Library of Congress Control Number: 2020904903

Book cover design by: Beverly Hurwitz

Interior design by: Katie Mullaly, Surrogate Press®

This book is dedicated to all of the patients and families
who have ever been doubted by unknowing doctors,
and to all of the doctors who make the mistake of assuming
the patient is crazy before assuming that they are ill.

Chapter One

"I've got Carol Farrell out in the waiting room with two of her kids and a screaming baby," Nina the ER admitting clerk warned. "Do you want me to bring them back?"

Triage nurse Liselle Grady slapped her own forehead. "Exactly what I don't need tonight. Which of the kids is she here for? Not Merrill, I hope."

"A new baby, a little girl with Harold's red hair. She looks like a robust healthy infant, but she's screaming loud enough to burst your eardrums."

"How long have they been here? Is Carol raging yet?"

"They got here about ten minutes ago and Carol looks pretty stressed out, even for Carol. The stupid registration computer is extra slow right now, and the waiting room is packed. Anyone without air conditioning is looking to spend some time where it's not roasting, even if it's in a hospital waiting room. We just registered a woman with a mole on her knee for nine years, but tonight, it's itchy."

"Some of our citizens will find whatever reason they can to get out of their sweltering apartments tonight," Liselle concurred. "Why does Carol want the baby seen?"

"She says the baby screams unconsolably and it's happening more frequently."

"So, has the baby been screaming all this time they're out there?"

"Actually, it was kind of weird. When Carol first came to the sign-in desk, the baby seemed calm, but she also seemed especially serious-looking for a four-month old. Leaning back in Carol's lap, she looked like she was studying everything around her. Then she looked directly at me and suddenly, her face contorted into this look of anguish and she just started screaming. Carol hugged her but she just screamed louder. Must be my freckly face," Nina lamented.

Liselle shook her head. "We love your freckly face around here, Nina, but Carol will probably be the one that screams if she sees my face. If Carol's in *our* ER, you can bet she's been in a few others before she'd ever come back here. She must be angrier at the other hospitals than she's angry with CityStar, and, there must be another crazy thing going on with another one of her poor kids.

"Nina, can I impose on you to check in with your cache of contacts in the other hospitals to see if someone will let us know if they've seen this baby, and if they can give us any helpful information? Carol probably won't tell us about all of her other medical encounters. I wonder who her pediatrician is these days, or if she's exhausted the entire city supply?"

"I'll see what I can dig up, Liselle. With all of the legal issues regarding this family, it might be hard to get anyone to talk, but I'll try. Meanwhile, is there any way to get them out of the waiting room? The screaming's unnerving everyone. You're not going to want the baby in a hallway either."

Liselle wiped some steam from her eyeglasses and pinned up her long black hair. The air conditioning seemed inadequate this hot humid night. "Is Harold or Merrill with Carol?"

"I didn't see either of them, but you never know who she's got stowed in the van, although it's probably too hot for anyone to be waiting in a vehicle. I think she's here with just the younger kids, but it's been about two years since I've seen any of them. Except for Merrill, I'm not sure I can tell any of the kids apart anymore, let alone remember which one is Cheryl, or Laurel or Beryl. By the way, the baby's name is Darryl."

"Why am I not surprised? Give me a few minutes. I've got a patient I can probably boot from room eight, and I'll send a nurse out to get them. And thanks for the warning, Nina. I'm really glad you're here tonight. I sure hope I've got the right doctor here tonight to deal with the likes of Carol Farrell."

Chapter Two

*D*r. Dewy Meadows dreaded her rotation as an intern in the ER. Her singular goal in life was to be a psychiatrist and heal wounded souls. The mere thought of sewing up lacerations or collecting sputum samples made her cringe, but to get optimal clinical experience, she was committed to training in a program that required her to spend her internship in the general practice of a big city hospital.

Of the six required rotations: internal medicine, pediatrics, ob-gyn, surgery, psychiatry and emergency medicine, emergency medicine was the one Dewy most feared, especially since it turned out to be her first rotation.

During her initial week in the ER, Dr. Dewy had merely shadowed the senior residents and attending physicians, learning how things were done. But now it was her second week, and she was expected to perform independently, seeking guidance only as necessary. She had a nightmare after finding out that her first 'day' of independent doctoring would be at night. Arriving at seven p.m., she introduced herself to the triage nurse, Liselle Grady.

Observing Dewy's boyish haircut and shimmering silver scrubs that looked a bit like a cat suit, along with her silver sequined sneakers, Liselle predicted the nightshift was going to take on a whole new vibe. Silver wasn't a great color on most people, but against Dewy's olive-toned and radiant complexion, it looked sensational.

"Aren't you that intern that speaks multiple languages?" Liselle asked. "Your reputation precedes you."

"I am," Dewy replied," but unfortunately, the language thing has turned into a problem. During my first week of internship, I got called all over the hospital to interpret, and my program director said, 'no more.' I'm here to learn medicine, not serve as a translator. Sorry! I can help if it doesn't take me away from my own patients."

"Makes sense to me," Liselle said, as she suddenly spun around and turned her back to Dewy, simultaneously grabbing Dewy's hand and pulling her into the privacy alcove behind the nursing station.

"Sorry about that," she explained to a visibly bewildered Dewy. "They just brought a patient back that I once had a bit of a run-in with. I thought it would be best if this particular patient doesn't know I'm the head nurse tonight."

Dewy's face had question marks all over it, and Liselle decided to see if this fresh young doctor might have what it takes to work with a hostile force like Carol Farrell. The attending physician on the schedule had been grumpy of late, the victim of a surprise divorce, and he also had a bad track record with Carol Farrell, as did the senior resident. It would be best to have someone who didn't have a history with this family to take on the case.

"Let me explain," Liselle said. "The patient I'm avoiding, the patient's mom that is, used to be a frequent flyer in our ER because her little boy Merrill has bad asthma. He was about eight years old when she kept bringing him in, not for the asthma, but for abdominal pain. His pediatrician had done all kinds of tests, but everything was normal.

"One night, Merrill showed up here just writhing in pain, but all of his labs and imaging were fine. The ER doctor opted for a psych evaluation because there was nothing else to explain the pain.

I wound up doing the consult because I had recently switched to ER nursing from being a psychiatric nurse for six years, and also because the psych resident was tied up with a suicidal patient, and she had two more waiting for her. Some nights are like that.

"The mom, Carol Farrell, was furious that no one was doing anything for her child, and after all the normal tests he'd had, I was worried that there was someone in the family doing something inappropriate to this kid. I got the insurer to agree to a diagnostic admission so we could use a surveillance camera to monitor family interaction. After three days in the hospital, the camera showed nothing inappropriate, but it did show that Merrill would have bouts of pain that would make him flail around and cry, and Carol would verbally pummel whoever was trying to take care of him.

"After upper and lower GI scoping was normal, our pediatric surgeon proposed doing an exploratory laparotomy, but Carol adamantly refused because she didn't want her son opened up by 'incompetent' doctors in search of a mystery. Then somehow, she noticed the hidden camera in the ceiling, and she went ballistic. She immediately yanked Merrill out of the hospital and started lawsuits against the hospital and our doctors and nurses.

"A few months later, we learned that Merrill had shown up in the University Hospital ER where an ultrasonographer thought she saw thickening of the gallbladder. Then it was realized that Merrill liked to kiss his kitties, in particular, a cat named Bravo that had recently died. Thinking he might be infected with the giardia parasite, even though his test was negative, and he'd never had the diarrhea that the parasite typically causes, he was treated with anti-parasite medicine, but it didn't help.

"Then, the dead cat clue prompted a GI doctor to scope Merrill's gallbladder, where they found cysts of the giardia parasite hiding in the gallbladder walls. Intensive IV anti-parasitic drugs also didn't help, so ultimately, they removed his gallbladder, which cured him. As I understand it, Mrs. Farrell has been suing all of the previous health care providers for missing this rare diagnosis. I'm just one of the seventeen defendants named in her lawsuits, and Dr. Patel and I and some others are also being sued for defamation of character."

Dr. Dewy Meadows shook her head. "Wow! I had no idea the giardia parasite could do that. I can really sympathize with that mother. That must have been horrible to have her child suffer like that, while the professionals were pointing fingers at her."

"The thing is, Dr. Meadows, if this mom loves her kids so much, why does she have a houseful of cats, while this same child frequently winds up hospitalized because he has bad allergic asthma? Not to mention he gets parasites from the cats. As a psych nurse, I totally understand that people cannot part with their beloved pets, but this little guy Merrill has suffered too much because his mother is a crazy cat woman.

"Aren't you doing a psychiatry residency? This could be an interesting case for you."

"But she's here for a crying baby? I'm not exactly expert in pediatrics."

"That's precisely why this is a good case for you. With crying infants, understanding what's going on is all about communicating with the parents. Other than a hot eardrum or tender belly, infants rarely give physicians any clues about what's bothering them. The senior resident tonight is Monica Stone. She'll back you up if you need help, and so will Dr. Patel.

"Welcome to our ER, Dr. Meadows. Here comes Gus the intake nurse. He's almost as new as you are, but so far, we think he's going to be super nurse. He's smart and studious, and he knows how to make people feel comfortable. I didn't tell him anything about Carol Farrell before I assigned him to the case."

Gus was the most handsome but tiny man Dewy had ever seen, barely five feet tall. Along with his wavy jet-black hair and finely chiseled features, his ocean blue eyes were outright alluring. At five foot seven, Dewy wished she could sit down at that moment, just to be eye to eye with his handsome face. After introductions, Gus presented the case.

"That's one upset mother in there. Geez, is she a talker, and that voice! So loud and shrill! Anyway, she says this baby, Darryl, is four-and-a-half months old, and she's been having screaming fits since she's nine weeks old. She was full-term, normal pregnancy and delivery, and there were no neonatal problems. They've been to a bunch of doctors and had numerous tests and treatments, but nothing is helping. Tonight, Darryl was screaming louder than ever, so that's why she felt she had to bring her in.

"At first, I could barely hear the mom because Darryl was screaming so loudly. Then she abruptly stopped, so I was able to get some vital signs, all normal. She's right in the middle of the growth curve and her motor development seems good for her age. I squeezed some urine out of her diaper, and it was okay on a dipstick. Mom says her BMs are soft and regular, but sometimes she screams when she poops.

"The mother also says she has a good appetite, but she'll stop in the middle of a feeding and just hysterically cry for a few minutes. Then she acts really hungry and finishes her bottle. Mom was initially breastfeeding, and she eliminated all the offending foods from her diet, but Darryl still cried with feedings, so they switched her to formula. Several formula changes also haven't helped. Now she's on medicine for reflux, but that isn't helping either.

"That poor baby! It sounds like something terrible is hurting her and you can see the frayed nerves in the mom and the other kids. There was a little boy in the same room, waiting for the orthopedist to set his broken arm. The baby's screaming was so unsettling, I moved the other child out into the hall."

Dewy looked skyward and rolled her head in a little circle when Liselle handed her Darryl Farrell's chart on a tablet. Gus volunteered to introduce her. Baby Darryl was quiet when they entered the room, though she seemed to be sweaty. Wasn't everyone on this hot, muggy night?

"This is Dr. Meadows," Gus said with his relaxing voice. "She's one of CityStar Hospital's best. I've shared with her what you've told me. I sure hope we can figure out poor Darryl's problem and get her and you some relief."

Chapter Three

The intense heat of the night was taking its toll on everyone. There were now sixteen patients in ten treatment rooms, five patients in the hallway, and the little boy in the hallway who was getting his broken arm set, was howling like a wolf. The doctors and nurses were visibly perspiring as they ran from room to room, and Dr. Brent Patel, the attending physician, seemed even grouchier than normal. He approached Liselle's desk with a scowl on his face and demanded to know where the new intern was.

'She's seeing one of Carol Farrell's kids, a new baby who cries a lot. I figure we'll find out what this young doctor is made of if she can manage Carol Farrell."

"OMG! Hopefully she survives." Dr. Patel scowled some more. "I was hoping she could help me with a Mandarin-speaking man with chest pain. I heard she speaks multiple languages."

"Well, everyone else heard about her too, and apparently took advantage. Now she's been restricted from serving as an interpreter. I'll see if there's someone on staff tonight who's certified for Mandarin and get the language service on the line for you if not. In the meantime, I'll check on Dr. Meadows to make sure she hasn't been eaten alive. She's been in that room more than fifteen minutes; too long, even for an intern."

Liselle was about to page Dr. Meadows when Nina returned from the waiting room and motioned Liselle back into the privacy alcove. "I got the scoop from my friend at Community General. The baby's been there twice. The first time, she was crying ferociously, and they did a skeletal survey to see if she might have a broken bone, but the x-rays were okay. The second time, she stopped crying as soon as they put her in a room. All she did was peacefully sleep. They did some basic labs, and everything was normal.

"I also got a buddy to look at her chart at University Hospital. She was there a few weeks ago, crying hysterically. They had to sedate her to examine her and they got an ophthalmology consult to make sure there wasn't a corneal abrasion or some other problem with her eyes. Everything was normal.

"I couldn't get a hold of anyone I know at Pine Meadow Medical Center."

"You're amazing, Nina. On the nights you're not here, it's just a goddamn guessing game. If only health care was about sharing important medical information instead of privacy. Imagine if all the computers talked to one another. We'd probably save hundreds of millions, and we could care for patients more efficiently if we weren't all repeating the labs and x-rays that were already done. Now that the lawyers have made such a mess out of health care with privacy rules, maybe all of the doctors should get together and reform the legal system.

"Here comes the intern I sent in to see Carol, poor woman, but she is still standing, and she looks to be in one piece." Liselle turned to Dr. Dewy Meadows. "So, how'd that go?"

Dr. Patel joined the conversation as Dewy said, "very interesting. The baby didn't cry the whole time I was in the room, and I was able to do a thorough exam, all perfectly normal. Eardrums clear, soft belly, no resistance to my manipulating her joints or squeezing her bones. No foreign bodies in her orifices that I could see.

"The mother on the other hand was just about bawling like a baby. She's at her wit's end with this infant's screaming and the inability of all the 'damn' doctors to figure out what's wrong. In addition to crying in the middle of feedings, she says that Darryl screams for a few minutes around six a.m., a few times a week, and none of them are getting much sleep. The crying is getting more frequent and for longer periods. It happens at least once or twice every day. None of her six other kids have been sick, but she did tell me that her son Merrill had a parasite in his gallbladder a few years ago, and that the baby's pediatrician did some testing to make sure the baby doesn't have something similar.

"When I asked about pets in the home, Carol kind of clammed up, but one of her daughters literally danced around the room reciting, almost singing, the names of her kitties. I had to write them down." Dewy looked at her tablet: "Babo, Bilbo, Bingo, Bluto, Bojo, Brillo, Bronco, and Bruno. Then the other little girl chimed in and said, 'no, Laurel, Brillo ran away.'

"Carol then asked me if I like cats. I'm actually a dog person but I lied and said I love cats. Then I told her about my 'cat' *Zareen*, which is Farsi for golden. Zareen was actually a beagle that my geologist stepfather swore could sniff out gold in a pile of rocks. After I raved about Zareen 'the kitty,' Carol willingly talked about her cats. She told me which ones live in the house and which ones are outdoor cats, which ones she got from the shelter and which ones she adopted out of boxes in front of the grocery store, which one had cancer, which was the favorite of which child, and more than I could ever care to know.

"Wow can that woman talk! I could hardly get a word in and her voice is like fingernails on a blackboard. Without my asking, Carol said all of the cats are up to date on their vaccines, and they're all healthy, nice cats. You know, she wasn't unpleasant until the cat issue came up, and then she got quite defensive.

"She's seen several doctors about the crying, and they did a bone scan in another ER. They're calling Darryl's problem colic, and they say she'll outgrow it. Carol's tried all kinds of colic remedies. Pacifiers, hot water bottles, massage, and swaddling haven't helped. Warm baths, rocking, and a chiropractic adjustment made the crying worse. She's also tried sugar water, herbal remedies, Tylenol, Advil, antacids, and now Darryl is on two reflux meds. This mom is so angry, that we're probably all fortunate that she didn't come in here with a weapon."

Liselle sympathized with Dewey's frustration and passed along the information about the skeletal x-rays and eye exam that she gleaned from Nina's clandestine networking. "So, what are you going to do with her?"

"Well, you were right about this being an interesting case, and I really appreciate that you gave me your perspective as a psychiatric nurse. Carol presents with a complex pattern of obsessive-compulsive disorder, characterized by her animal hoarding, her obsession with the health issues of her kids and cats, and the ritualistic naming thing.

"I just happen to know about ritualistic naming. I was born Dewy Fields and after my dad died; my mom chose to marry a man with the last name of Meadows. She named my sisters Daisy and Dahlia. Somewhat like my mom, whose name is Carolena, this Carol is quite OCD."

Nurse Liselle and Dr. Patel exchanged furtive glances in response to Dewy's comments. "Well, yes, Carol *is* an interesting case," Liselle said, "but what are you going to do about the patient, the crying baby? I can assure you that Carol is not going to be amenable to any form of psychiatric intervention."

Dr. Patel agreed and as he took off to attend to another gasping asthmatic, he remarked, "something bad in the air tonight; they're all wheezing."

Liselle said, "Carol actually doesn't fit the pattern of an animal hoarder, Dr. Meadows, in that she seems to take very good care of her cats. When we were dealing with Merrill's asthma, we were able to communicate with her vet's office. The cats were all getting annual check-ups, and the vet told our social worker that Carol tended to hysterics if any of the cats were sick, demanding that something be done, even when there was nothing left to do.

"When we had her residence checked out by animal control, I should say her mansion, it was reported that everything there was exceptionally tidy, and there were a few well-tended cat graves in the backyard. She's a very interesting case all right, but not your case, Dr. Meadows. Your case is the crying baby.

"Please present the baby's case to Dr. Stone as soon as she comes out of room seven. She's had prior experience with this family. In the meantime, I need you to quick see the man in the first bed in the hallway. He just needs someone to listen to his lungs and order a breathing treatment. That shouldn't take you more than five minutes. When we're this busy, you have to totally limit your hand-holding."

Dr. Monica Stone seemed old to be a resident. Dewy would later learn that she had been a nurse for twelve years before she went to medical school, so she had much more clinical experience than most doctors in training. She was sympathetic about Dewy landing such a tough case on her first solo stint.

Having recently seen the case of a patient with sudden bouts of pain caused by a tumor that squirts adrenalin, Dr. Stone suggested testing for adrenalin-related hormones in the baby's urine.

The tumor, called *pheo-chromo-cy-toma*, was often too tiny to be seen on imaging, so diagnosis depended on measurement of certain chemicals in the urine over a twenty-four-hour period. To get accurate test results in a baby required placement of a catheter into the bladder or catching every drop of urine in special bags taped to the skin. Darryl's case didn't warrant admission, so they'd have to keep her in the ER to get the test done.

Dr. Monica also suggested resting the baby's stomach and supporting her with intravenous nutrition to see if that eliminated the screaming.

Carol Farrell vehemently objected when Dewy explained about testing for the tumor. "That's ridiculous! I have a lot of kids and kitties to take care of. I can't stay here for twenty-four hours. There's no way I'm letting you stick a catheter in my daughter's bladder. Why don't you give me the baggies and a container? I'll do the collecting at home and bring the urine back tomorrow. This baby is miserable enough. I'm not going to let you bastards torture her."

"I'm so sorry, Mrs. Farrell, but there are a few reasons we want to keep Darryl here. Number one, we want to monitor her vital signs when she has her crying spells. Secondly, we want to put her on IV nutrition and give her a rest from oral feeding to see if that eliminates the crying. Thirdly, these urine bags need constant monitoring and changing. If some of the urine spills, the test results are invalid. So, if this test is worth doing, let's do it right.

"And lastly, you need to get some sleep yourself, so I'm ordering a cot for you."

After letting go a tirade of vitriol, Carol's anger morphed into acquiescence. She said she'd call her mother to come get the other kids and fill in for her at home. "I'm not going to leave my baby here alone in this hell hole. My insurer is probably going to pay a gazillion dollars for this stupid test to be done in an ER, and you damn doctors better get this right."

Dr. Dewy Meadows was so taken back by Carol's hostile demeanor, that she suddenly questioned her desire to be a psychiatrist, and maybe even to be a doctor. It really was all about taking care of people at their worst.

Chapter Four

M olly Hudson groaned as she put down her phone.

"What's the matter now?" her husband George asked.

"It's Carol again. She's at CityStar Hospital with Darryl because the screaming got really bad this evening. They want to keep the baby there for twenty-four hours to do some kind of test, and Carol hates that place and doesn't want to just leave her there. She needs me to pick up Laurel and Beryl and sleep over at their house to get them off to camp in the morning."

"Why on earth did she take the other kids with her?"

"Because Cheryl wasn't there to babysit, and Harold's always overwhelmed if he has to take care of the little ones. Cheryl's been spending more time at a friend's house, and who can blame her with the baby screaming like that?"

"Yeah! Harold's only good at making babies, not tending them, and poor Cheryl doesn't really need to be used as the perpetual babysitter. Do you think your daughter will ever stop having babies?"

"I wish I knew the answer to that, George, but Carol is who she is. It's truly a miracle she even has a husband; and Harold, for all of his faults, is a wonderful provider. I just wish they had some friends who could help them out once in a while, cause I'm getting too old for this."

"No you're not, Molly. You're a great grandma and those kids are doing as well as they are because of you. I can't even imagine what they'd be like if Carol and Harold were the only adults in their lives."

George observed Molly to be on the verge of tears as she packed an overnight bag. He took her in his arms as she sobbed, "It's never going to end for me, George. Carol is thirty-six years old and I'm going to be her only friend for the rest of my life. Besides Harold, I seem to be the only person on Earth who can stand her, and I can barely stand her. Her father divorced us both when she was eight, because he couldn't stand her relentless jabbering and griping.

"You know, I was just thinking, when Carol was in third grade, she actually had a friend, a little boy named Jaime. Just like Harold, Jaime hardly talked at all, and for some reason, he didn't walk away when Carol would go on and on with her blathering. It was so strange to watch them play together. Carol would narrate everything they did, and Jaime would just take orders from her and shake his head yes at whatever she said. But Jaime's family moved away after fourth grade, and until Harold came along, Carol was virtually friendless."

"Did she date before Harold?" George asked. "With that baby doll face of hers, I can't imagine the guys weren't interested."

"Well, not in high school. She was too well known as an intolerable yackaholic by junior high. Good student that she was, even her teachers never wanted to engage with her. When she first got to college, she got asked out on lots of dates, but never for a second date. I don't think she had any more dates after her freshman year, and I don't think she'd have ever found a husband if she hadn't been hired as an accountant for Harold's dental lab.

"I still remember the day that Harold asked her out on a second date. Her sister and I were so amazed that we had a little celebration dinner and got drunk. I've never told anyone that before. While my relationship with Carol was tough, her sister Judy and I were close. I think we were kind of bound together in our misery of having to live with Carol. Gee whiz, I miss Judy, but I can't blame her for moving as far away as she did. If my conscience would let me, I'd move as far away from Carol as I could too. What do you think about living in Hawaii?"

"You know you could never do that, Molly. You are too devoted a grandparent and your grandbabies need you. In spite of their whacko parents and quirkiness, those kids all seem to have good potential.

"Even grouchy Terrell seems to be maturing into a good kid because of you, and now, that poor little baby needs your help. I just hope the doctors can get to the bottom of what's making her scream like that. Just one afternoon at their house was enough to make me want to run away. I admire Carol's perseverance in trying to find an answer. I don't know anything about colic, but I don't know how anyone can deal with an infant screaming like that."

"Carol was a colicky baby too; so was Gerald, and especially, so was Terrell," Molly reminisced, "but I don't remember any of them ever screaming like that. And, like the doctors kept saying, Terrell outgrew his colic by the time he was five months old, though he was still an irritable baby. Now he's an irritable twelve-year-old, but he's a good student and he seems to have some of Harold's mechanical talent. I used to like watching him make things with his Legos. I bet he winds up making false teeth like his father. Terrell would just rather be around things than people."

"Or cats." George added. "It's so interesting how Merrill adores those cats, while Terrell and Gerald seem to hate them. I think Harold just tolerates the cats.

"By the way, is Harold still planning to open another dental lab? I can't imagine how much more luxurious their lives will be if he doubles his already fat income, except that sending seven kids to college will cost a bundle. And, I do wonder if they'll ever stop having babies."

"I don't think either of them have said anything about the second lab since Darryl was born. They're probably just too preoccupied with her problem to be making business decisions. Maybe Darryl will keep them from working on baby number eight."

"Hey, it's getting late. You better get over to CityStar and get those kids home to bed. Do you want me to come with you?"

"Thanks, George. I'll be all right by myself and you have to do that orientation tomorrow for the new faculty. At least I won't have to deal with Carol and that poor unhappy baby once I get there, and Harold's always pleasant and appreciative when I'm there. I'm so grateful for that. In his own way, he really is a sweetheart."

Chapter Five

When Molly arrived at the Farrell household at ten-thirty p.m., three of her grandchildren were still awake. The little girls, Laurel and Beryl, had both fallen asleep in the car after she picked them up at the ER, and with Harold's help, both were now snuggled in their beds. They had to displace a couple of cats from Laurel's bed to make room for her. Little Laurel seemed to have all of the makings of a future cat-lady.

Ten-year-old Merrill was also sound asleep and cuddled up with a cat, but adolescents Cheryl and Terrell were wide awake and worried about their baby sister and they wanted to know what was going on.

Meanwhile, seven-year-old "Gyro" Gerald, as usual, was bouncing off the walls. That child seemed to never need sleep, and the medicine they were giving him for hyperactivity only made him more sleepless.

Molly wasn't even there for twenty minutes when Harold headed off to bed. His mother-in-law sympathized. Harold worked twelve-hour days and then he typically roughhoused with the kids when he got home. Although his routine seemed physically exhausting, Molly figured it was probably less tiring for him to play with the kids all evening than to sit and listen to Carol's endless details of what the kids and kitties had been doing all day.

On weekends, Harold would take the older kids bowling, swimming, hiking, or just out for a car ride. Molly wondered if he kept making babies so he could leave the young ones home with Carol, while hanging out with the older kids gave him an acceptable escape route. Still, she couldn't fathom why Carol wanted to keep making babies. Although she obsessively took good care of all of them, she wasn't particularly attached to any of them.

It was miraculous, Molly thought, that except for Laurel and Gerald, the kids seemed to have mostly inherited Harold's Asperger's traits, rather than Carol's unique form of nuttiness. Only seven-year-old Gerald appeared to be a yackaholic like his mother. He tended to scare other kids away with his perpetual prattling and physical fidgeting. Even the cats avoided him.

Molly wondered if Laurel might also turn out to be a chatterbox. Super-smart little Laurel was already reading at age four, but so like her mother at that age, Laurel spent most of her time playing with and talking to the cats.

Fourteen-year-old Cheryl, and ten-year-old Merrill, were reserved and quiet like their father, but they both seemed to be able to maintain friendships, while twelve-year-old Terrell seemed like a loner. Poor Terrell had probably inherited the worst traits of both of his parents. Although he was very bright, he was socially awkward and almost always ornery.

Beryl seemed to have gotten the best mix of her parent's genes. At that wonderful age of six, bubbly Beryl reminded Molly of her daughter Judy at that age, except that when Judy was six, four-year-old Carol's relentless babbling had started driving her into escapism.

"So, what do they think is wrong with the baby?" Big Sister Cheryl asked her grandmother. "Is she going to be okay? Why can't they help her? I've never seen that poor little baby smile or look happy, not even once."

"Yeah, why can't they make her stop crying? I can't stand listening to her cry," Terrell said. "It's driving me crazy and it's making Mommy extra crazy."

"It really is awful," echoed Cheryl, "especially at six in the morning. I don't think any of us have had a decent night's sleep this whole week. Sometimes my heart goes hippity-hop when Darryl starts to scream."

"Well, maybe they'll figure out how to help Darryl after they get these tests done."

"I hope it doesn't take as long for them to figure out what's wrong with Darryl as it did when Merrill was sick." Cheryl said. "He was really sick, for almost a year before they figured out what was wrong. It was terrible. He'd be up crying in the middle of the night and Mommy and Daddy couldn't help him and neither could any of the doctors."

"And he lost a lot of weight," Terrell added, squeezing his own little roll of prepubescent belly fat.

"But Merrill's fine now. They did figure it out and they got him all better." Molly tried to reassure her grandchildren, as she gently removed her foot out from under a curled-up cat. "Doctors always try to figure out what's wrong with their patients, but sometimes it takes a lot of time for the illness to show its true self, and a baby can't even tell them what hurts. Merrill had a very unusual illness. He was actually very lucky that the doctors did ultimately figure it out and they were able to cure him. Medicine isn't a perfect science like math."

"I'm really loving algebra, Grandma. I think I want to be a math professor like you," Cheryl said.

Terrell changed the subject back to Merrill's illness. "It was that sick cat Bravo that got him sick. Mommy ought to get rid of these cats. They made Merrill really sick and they're all over the place. She loves those cats more than she loves Merrill."

"That's not true." Molly said, feeling a pang of guilt, because she had said the same thing to Carol on multiple occasions. She wondered if Terrell had overheard her say it some time. He was the kind of kid who lurked in the shadows.

"Your mother does love her kitties, but she loves each of you children very much. I think it's because she loves children so much that she has so many children. You kids also have a very good daddy. You're very lucky to be part of a great big, loving family. There are people who don't have two parents, or sisters and brothers, or pets, and they have to face the world all by themselves.

"I'm going to tell you kids a secret. You have to promise to not tell Mommy I told you. When your mother was a little girl, she had a best friend named Jaime. They were truly good buddies and they played together almost every day. But then, Jaime's family moved far away, and there weren't other kids around for your mother to play with. She was so lonely that she started to spend all of her time with her kitty, Briko. She'd talk to Briko for hours and hours and that cat was a good listener. Then, one day she found a stray cat and brought it home. It was all white and we named her Blanco, and your mother would talk to Blanco all the time too. We found out later that Blanco was deaf, but to your Mommy, the cats were her best friends. She loves you children, but she also loves her best friends.

"Now you kids need to go to bed, and let's hope you can finally get a good night's sleep while the doctors try to help Baby Darryl. But first, Terrell, I need you to help me carry Gerald to bed. I think he finally conked out in the playroom."

Chapter Six

At two a.m., the heat gave way to intense thunderstorms, and except for some auto accident victims, the flow of patients had considerably slowed. By five a.m., things had settled enough for Dr. Patel to be able to review the charts of the new intern. She was really slow moving, but she seemed to be very competent. He was struck by the fact that her case summaries always started with a psychologic assessment:

This is a seventeen-year-old student complaining of a headache for three days. She seems anxious and has a pressured speech pattern.

This is a forty-year-old laborer who presents for knee pain that started today without an identifiable precipitant. He frequently expresses self-depreciation and appears depressed.

Dr. Patel could usually tell which of the new interns was headed for a psychiatry career, because they tended to wear their personal pain on their sleeve. Dr. Dewy Meadows didn't seem to fit that picture though. She appeared to be a basically upbeat person, yet her notes were a dead give-away as to her future specialty.

She certainly seemed to have good clinical judgment, correctly diagnosing some pathology that could easily be missed. Brent Patel was relieved that she had so far survived her interactions with Carol Farrell, even though she'd gone back into the room to check on the baby multiple times.

Last he'd heard, both Carol and the baby were sleeping, and he was grateful that there had yet to be a major scene because they weren't doing enough for the crying baby. During his career at CityStar, he had seen Merrill Farrell for severe asthma attacks on multiple occasions, and Carol was one of the most challenging people he had ever dealt with. She was a ferocious advocate for her kids, except for the cat thing. Dr. Patel considered the cat thing to be a sick form of child abuse, but the hospital social workers all agreed that no judge in the family court system would take Merrill away from his strong-willed mother and her cats.

Dr. Brent Patel was so concerned about Merrill that he had even consulted with a child welfare attorney about the case. "There are just too many solid arguments against forced removal of pets," the lawyer counseled. "First of all, there's the fact that unless a parent wants their child to live in a bubble for the rest of their life, that child will be exposed to cat dander wherever they go. People with cat dander on their clothing leave the allergen on furnishings and it gets into the air ducts of every school, workplace, church, theater and store in the world. Even hospital air is full of cat and dog dander.

"Secondly, having a cat in the home, seems to help build immunity to cat dander. Thirdly, there's a growing body of evidence that shows that children who grow up with pets in their homes are healthier than pet-less kids. And finally, removing a cherished pet from the home can cause major emotional distress. Neither science nor the law is on Merrill's side, I'm sorry to say. The best you can do is try to get the parents to create a cat-free zone for this kid within the home and put an air filter in his bedroom."

They had already done all of that, but they had no success in keeping Merrill from kissing his kitties. The cats loved this child and he loved them back. A social work student who visited the Farrells in their home had even reported seeing Merrill walk around the house with a tuxedo cat named Bravo draped over his shoulders.

Dr. Patel found himself feeling a little bit jealous when he read Dewy's notes about a man who was brought in by a tourist service for sudden onset of confusion. Apparently, because she was fluent in Farsi, she was able to directly communicate with this patient who she noted to be an Afghani widower living in France. He was sightseeing in America with a tour group and a French-speaking tour guide, though his French was somewhat limited.

Speaking his native language, Dewy concluded that the man had accidentally taken an extra dose of his blood pressure medicines, causing him to become light-headed and disoriented. Had she not been his doctor, he probably would have been subjected to brain imaging and other expensive unnecessary tests.

Communication was a really important factor in being a diagnostician, and this young doctor had a truly enviable advantage over the rest of the physicians because of her linguistic ability. Dr. Patel was curious about her and hoped there'd be enough break time to actually converse with the new intern.

Then, around six a.m., three things happened to dash that hope. An ambulance arrived with two seriously injured car accident victims, another ambulance delivered a patient with a gunshot wound to the chest, and the Farrell baby started screaming like it was the end of the world. Seconds later, Carol was out in the hallway screaming that someone needed to do something for her baby.

Chapter Seven

*D*r. Dewy Meadows had just finished signing her patients over to the day shift and was on her way out, when Dr. Patel intercepted her. "You did a really excellent job on your first solo night," he said. "Do you have the energy to talk about your cases with me over breakfast?"

Dewy didn't think she had the energy to even eat or take a shower before trying to sleep, but she didn't want to say no to the attending physician. She felt too grubby to be near anyone, but Dr. Patel also looked like he needed a shower and a shave, and definitely, a change of his blood-spattered scrubs. They buttoned up their white coats to conceal their ER stains and headed to the hospital cafeteria. Dewy ordered a decaf and a bagel. Brent Patel, skinny man that he was, ordered the grand slam breakfast with a double espresso. It made Dewy uncomfortable when he insisted on paying for her order.

"Aren't you worried the coffee will keep you awake?" she asked as they sat down.

"I'm off for the next four days and I have a bunch of stuff to get done today, so I need the caffeine. As you'll come to learn, our schedule for the ER docs is three fourteen-hour night shifts a week, alternating with four ten-hour day shifts every other week. It's brutal to go from sleeping nights one week to sleeping days the next, but most of us like that we have three or four days out of the hospital on a weekly basis.

"You interns have a new schedule this year: three night shifts, two days off, six dayshifts, two days off. We'll see if it broadens your experience because you'll work with a wider range of mentors. Hopefully, it's more tolerable than the old schedule. Those who can't make the sleep adjustments really suffer, but even for those who can adapt, the ER schedule is hard on families. My wife got so sick of telling the kids 'be quiet, Daddy's sleeping,' that for the past year, I've stayed in the hospital and slept in a call room when I have to work the nightshift. I get woken up here a little less often than at home."

"Ay caramba," Dewy remarked in Spanish. "That's as good a reason as any to not go into emergency medicine. I've never been able to sleep during the day, so it's going to be a challenge for me to get through this rotation.

"So, how old are your kids?" Dewy asked.

"My little boy is four and my daughter is two." He took out his phone to show her a picture. Dewy was struck by how different looking the kids were. The little boy had his father's dark complexion and big brown eyes. The little girl was very blonde.

"How adorable!" Dewy was about to ask if their mother was blonde, but something made her decide not to pry. "It must be really hard to live with that constantly changing schedule. How long have you been at CityStar, Dr. Patel?"

"Please call me Brent. I've been in this ER for six years and before I came here, I worked in a small ER in a small town in Ohio for three years. That's where I met my wife. She was an ER nurse, so I thought she'd appreciate the crazy hours of an ER doctor. From a medical perspective, I much prefer the action in the big city hospital, but from a family perspective, I kind of wish I'd stayed in the small town.

"So, I have to ask you, Dewy, how did you come to speak so many languages? I was really impressed by how you handled the case of the confused tourist."

"So, here's my story. I'm fairly fluent in eight languages. My biologic father, Karl Fields, grew up in Pittsburg in a bilingual home with a German-speaking mother. He was fluent in German, and then because of his career, he learned to speak Farsi. He was a geologist and he worked for a company that gets consulted by miners and oil drillers from around the world. Some of his assignments were in Tajikistan and Uzbekistan; so that's why he learned Farsi.

"My mother, Carolena Shursky-Fields-Meadows, grew up in Miami with a Spanish-speaking mother and a Russian-speaking father. She was fluent in both, but she always considered English to be her primary language. In high school, she studied French and in college, she majored in French and Mandarin. The same company my father worked for hired her to serve as a translator for their international clients. That's how my parents met and that's when my mother learned Farsi.

"My mother was determined to have her kids be multilingual, so on Mondays, she only spoke to us in Mandarin. Tuesdays were for Spanish, Wednesdays Russian, Thursdays French, Fridays Farsi, Saturdays English, and on Sundays, she'd make my father talk to us in German. You might say my sister Daisy and I were a successful experiment. We were both fairly fluent in seven languages by the time we got to first grade.

"When I was four, my father got assigned to a project in South Korea. It was a huge project and he was scheduled to be there for a long time, so he moved us all to Korea. We were there for sixteen months and I attended nursery school where I learned Korean. I can't read or write in Mandarin, Korean, or Farsi, but I can comfortably converse.

"Then we moved back to the States because my father was consulting for an expanding mining company in Idaho. He was in a helicopter, exploring some mountainous terrain, when a sudden storm popped up and the copter crashed. There were no survivors."

"So sorry," Dr. Patel responded.

"Thanks. My mother very quickly married one of the other geologists that worked for the company. You might say my fathers were gold miners and my mother is a gold digger. My stepfather, Dave Meadows, adopted Daisy and me, so, I went from being Dewy Fields to Dewy Meadows. Daddy Dave doesn't speak any languages other than a little Arabic for his work.

"Then they had my stepsister Dahlia. She missed out on the linguistic genes. Just as Daisy and I were raised, Dahlia was spoken to in all of those languages, but by the time she was three, no matter what language we talked to her in, she always responded in English. She failed Carolena's experiment, but she did get some artistic genes from somewhere, and now she's studying design at the Fashion Institute of Technology in New York."

"What did your other sister do with her language skills?"

"Daisy majored in language in college, and learned Italian, Japanese and Hindi. She now works as a tour guide at the U.N. Last year, she married another linguist, so we can't wait to see how many languages her kids will speak, if she ever has kids. Right now, she and her husband are too busy attending parties for visiting dignitaries. When you're as multilingual as we are, you kind of become a party trick."

"This is so intriguing, Dewy," Brent said. "What language do you think in?"

"It very much depends on my mood and the circumstances. Sometimes, I start thinking in English, but my mind will grab a Mandarin or Korean word because it's more relevant or precise. Russian seems fitting when my thoughts are melancholy, and German pops into my head when I'm frustrated. When I'm pensive, shall we say *meditatif*, I tend to think in French. Romantic thoughts often play out in Spanish. My brain frequently translates song lyrics into Spanish because it's so much more melodic than the other languages. But, when I dream, I mostly dream in English. I mostly read in English and I prefer American music.

"Do you speak any foreign languages, Dr. Patel? Brent?"

"I wish! My father's parents spoke Bengali, and I think I can still understand it a little, but I can't speak it. My parents raised me to be an American boy and in our home, we spoke only English. I took three years of Spanish in high school, but I typically can't understand the dialects of the many Spanish-speaking patients that show up in our ER. I usually have to call for an interpreter, and sometimes the interpreters struggle with some of the dialects.

"You have excellent medical skills, Dewy. I'm curious as to why you're heading for psychiatry, but that's a story for another day. Right now, I think you need to get some sleep. You're going to have to face Carol Farrell when you get back tonight, so you better be feeling strong. By the way, did you get any clues when the baby started to scream this morning?"

"Not at all. Her heart rate monitor just showed the rapid rate you'd expect with her hysteria, and the machine had trouble reading everything because her screaming causes her whole little body to shudder.

"Her mother was also making a racket and demanding we do something, so Dr. Stone ordered a tiny dose of morphine to be added to her IV. Within two minutes of the morphine going in, the poor little thing stopped screaming. Now we don't know if the morphine helped, or if that was just the end point of her screaming spell.

"I know the mom is a real problem around here, but I truly sympathize with her. Hearing that baby scream like that was one of the hardest things I've ever had to do, and I only did it for a few minutes. It was just awful. Have you ever seen a case like this, Brent?"

"Oh, I've seen lots of screaming babies. Probably nine out of ten have an identifiable source of pain, if not colic, but then there's always that one that leaves you stumped.

"I'll never forget the mother who came back to the ER five times in two days because her perfectly healthy baby wouldn't stop crying. On the fifth visit, an observant nurse noticed the infant's little toe looked puffy and felt cold. With a magnifying glass, we found one of Mom's fine blonde hairs wrapped around the base of the toe, tight enough to act like a tourniquet and cause ischemic pain. The skin was so swollen that we couldn't safely grab the hair with forceps to cut it off. Then, while we doctors scratched our heads, our brilliant nurse showed up with a bottle of Nair that she sent a clerk to the drugstore to buy. She painted the little toe with the hair removal lotion and in five minutes, the hair dissolved, the toe pinked up, and that poor baby stopped crying.

"Most ERs now keep Nair on hand because hair tourniquets on baby appendages are not uncommon. Our nurses are all trained to check crying babies for this possibility. Last Christmas, there was a very unhappy infant here with a hair tourniquet around his penis, poor thing. Sometimes the tourniquet turns out to be a blanket fiber, which we figure out when Nair doesn't work. That's a much tougher problem."

"Dewy, I've got lots of stories to tell you about crying babies with mysterious ailments, but none of those cases share the added element of this uniquely difficult mother. Your department chairman can tell you more about Carol Farrell. Why don't you try to speak with Dr. Ortiz about her?

"As for trying to help that baby, and assuming she doesn't have an adrenalin squirting tumor, your most important task is going to be to get Carol to sign for consents for us to get the records of all the other providers that she's probably taken this child to. And then, we have to get one of our staff pediatricians to be willing to take on the case. Carol doesn't like to share that information and I don't think it's because she's malicious. I think it's because she so strongly distrusts doctors. You've got a really hard job ahead of you, Dewy. Go home and get some shuteye."

Chapter Eight

Molly Hudson was awakened by "Gyro" Gerald jumping onto her bed at six-thirty a.m. He was always up before Harold left for the lab at six, and Harold didn't seem to mind eating breakfast with Gerald jabbering away. Now, the little boy was rambling on about a birthday party at camp, and Molly tried to patiently listen to his gibberish for ten minutes before giving up. She shuffled him off to the playroom, got dressed and went downstairs to greet the housekeeper, who typically arrived a little before seven.

Molly was amazed that this particular housekeeper had already lasted nineteen months. Six months was the previous record, and many hadn't even lasted six weeks. When Carol and Harold first purchased the ten-bedroom, twelve-bath monstrosity, Carol planned to take care of it all herself. Her plan dissolved as soon as Merrill came home from the hospital, after spending seven weeks on a ventilator in neonatal intensive care because he was born prematurely.

Between Carol's obsession with tidiness, super shy four-year-old Cheryl hiding under her skirt most of the time, irritable Terrell in the middle of his terrible twos, a sick cat needing medicine three times a day, and Baby Merrill wheezing, coughing and needing frequent feedings and breathing treatments, Carol admitted to needing help.

The first housekeeper was there for one day. She left in tears when she was badly scratched by one of the cats. Molly couldn't recall how many cats there were back then, maybe just three or four. Then, an older woman lasted for five weeks before Carol verbally assaulted her for losing the baby's medicine syringe. Molly came over to help out the next day and by chance, found the syringe in one of the cat's beds. She confronted Carol about letting the cats walk on the counter where Merrill's medicine was kept, to no avail. A week later, that cat drank a medicine cup containing the baby's Tylenol, and by the next day, it was a dead cat.

Other housekeepers departed because the house was too big, or so they said. Agencies stopped sending Carol candidates, so she tried to hire mother's helpers from foreign countries. Molly worried that some of those young women were possibly human trafficking victims. Yet, for all of the hardship they'd maybe endured, trying to please Carol was too much for all of them. Carol had fired a few, while most had formally quit or simply never returned. The housekeeper memories prompted Molly to wonder how Tia had survived for this long.

She found Tia making oatmeal and pancakes and listening to Gerald's ranting about the camp birthday party. She said "good morning" three times before the sprightly older woman turned around, looking stunned.

"You're not Mrs. Farrell! I'm sorry, Grandma Molly, you startled me."

"Carol's at CityStar Hospital with the baby. The crying got much worse last evening and they're doing some special testing. Hopefully, they'll get home tonight and I'll stay with the kids until they get here. I'll go get them dressed for camp. So, is Beryl still restricting her breakfast to doughnut holes?"

"Beryl eats oatmeal now, as long as there's no raisins in it. She's actually turning into the best eater of the bunch. I don't know how

Terrell survives on his diet. Though he'll sometimes eat my pancakes, he's mostly eating pop tarts and cheese doodles. And why not, when his mother buys him tons of that garbage?

"Laurel gives most of her food to the cats, so I'm not sure what she actually eats. Where's Gerald? I've got his corn flakes ready. He was just here."

"I'll track him down, Tia. Don't add the milk yet. I want to get him mosquito-proofed because Carol said his counselor is taking his group hiking today, and after all that rain last night, Gerald will get eaten alive. That child is just a flashing neon 'diner' sign for mosquitos. Are their bathing suits in the laundry room? It's not supposed to be so hot today, but I'm sure they'll still go swimming."

"I'll pack up their backpacks while you round them up. Please tell Terrell and Merrill their pancakes are ready. Would you like pancakes too, or I can fix you an omelet? I usually make Cheryl an omelet if she's even in the mood for breakfast, but she's been sleeping later and later, so I'm not sure when that will be. When my kids were in their teen growth spurts, they couldn't eat enough or sleep enough."

With Tia's help, Molly managed to have Terrell, Merrill, Gerald, Beryl and Laurel fed, packed up and out on the driveway, waiting for the camp bus by eight-thirty. With the cats fed, Cheryl still sleeping, and Tia not yet on her bathroom/litter box cleaning circuit, Molly seized the opportunity to have a conversation with this wonder woman. Knowing Tia had much to do, she decided to get right to the point.

"So how do you do it, Tia? Where do you get the stamina to keep this monstrous house clean, tend all of the children and cats, and put up with my daughter's endless demands?"

"It's easy to love the children, Mrs. Hudson. They behave really well for me. Even Terrell never talks back to me the way he does with his mama.

"As for the cleaning, it's a piece of cake compared to how it was when I raised three kids in Belize in two rooms without electricity or running water. Five minutes in each of twelve bathrooms here takes me about an hour. In Belize, it took me more than an hour to haul enough water into my house to fix meals, clean the pots and clean the kids.

"My Belize house didn't have a bathroom. We shared an outhouse with another family. And, we depended on our cat to keep the vermin out. Now, because of the generous salary the Farrells are paying me, my grandchildren in Belize will have a much better life."

"I can't even imagine that, Tia. Still, I'm amazed that Carol doesn't get on your nerves, especially with all the stress being created here by that poor screaming baby."

Tia's sun-crinkled face broke into a sly smile. "I'll share a secret with you, Mrs. Hudson, just between you and me. Even the children don't know."

Tia pulled back her thick gray hair to reveal hearing aids on both sides. "When Mrs. Farrell goes on a rampage, I just turn my hearing aids off and nod. Before I started working here, I couldn't afford hearing aids, and like most folks who've lost their hearing, my brain just learned to shut out all the background noise. My brain's learned to do the same with Mrs. Farrell. It's kind of a handy disability. And I really have come to love the children and I want to help them. It's so hard for them to deal with their mother's constant chiding. I just wish someone could help that poor unhappy baby."

"You're a godsend, Tia. I don't know if Carol and Harold appreciate you, but I'm very grateful for how positive an impact you've had on the kids. I can see the difference in all of them. Thanks for being here and for sharing your secret with me. I'd love to know more about your family, but you have a ton of work to do and I have to attend a curriculum meeting this morning, so I'll let you get to work, and I'll go do mine.

"I'll be back by two to take Cheryl to the orthodontist. George and I will take the kids out for pizza tonight; so, don't worry about fixing dinner for them. You have a good day."

Chapter Nine

E ven though her studio apartment was on the eleventh floor of the hospital-housing complex, the noise from the city streets made it hard for Dewy to sleep. She spent some time reading about adrenal gland tumors before finally closing her eyes. She managed to sleep a good six hours before being awakened by a loud boom, followed by blaring sirens. She wouldn't learn until the next morning's news that the explosion was caused by someone dropping a firecracker into the mailbox on the street corner; just another stupid prank in the big city.

After reading some more and eating a frozen dinner, she decided to get to the hospital ahead of her shift to see what was going on with the Farrells. She couldn't get them off her mind, or as she thought in Mandarin, they had her *danxin*.

At six-thirty p.m., the ER was bustling. A resuscitation was in progress, and an ambulance had just delivered car crash victims. Almost everyone was tied up with the code and the traumas. The only person who Dewy managed to corner was the triage nurse, a seriously tattooed, bejeweled bald man, named Xavier Rayburn, who everyone called "Xray" or just plain "X". Dewy had met Xray on her first day in the ER when he gave the new interns and the medical and nursing students their orientation. She learned a lot from him, and thoroughly enjoyed his dry sense of humor.

"Hey, hey, Dewy 'Silver Tongue,' I heard they're not going to let you be our interpreter anymore. Too bad! It was so convenient to have that kind of help here last week. Sorry to learn you drew the night shift and Carol Farrell, you lucky girl.

"I think Carol's going to be happy to see you though, because she sure doesn't like the dayshift doctors. The only doc on today's shift who she hasn't terrorized in the past was the intern. He seems like a player, so I sent him in there, but he's got such a baby face that he looks like he's fifteen. Right after he did morning rounds, Carol came stomping down the hall and protesting that she wanted her child taken care of by a real doctor, not some junior high kid. And she's not the only one who's reacted that way to 'Dr. Babyface Brody'. I don't think this guy can even grow a beard if he tries, so I'm going to buy him a fake one."

Dewey flicked at her pixie bangs. "Wait until Carol realizes I'm also an intern. That's probably not going to go down well with her either. When you pick up the beard, see if you can get me a gray wig with a bun.

"So, what's been happening with the baby?"

"Nothing much. I heard she had a brutal screaming fit early this morning, but nothing on the dayshift. Every time she pees, Carol comes storming out of the room to demand that someone get in there and immediately change the bag. Until about an hour ago, I had a nursing student here who was doing an excellent job of pee bag changing, but until the traumas are all stabilized, I'm going to have to assign that job to you, you lucky girl." Xray grinned and returned his attention to triage.

Dewy turned down the hallway just in time to see the defeated faces and postures of Dr. Olga Volkov and the code team, emerging from room one. She stopped to observe. She had shadowed Dr. Olga during her first week in the ER and had enjoyed being able to chat with her in Russian. Now her mentor looked very somber and one of the nurses was in tears.

Dr. Volkov put her hand on the nurse's arm. "We had no chance in there, Hana. She was probably underwater much too long to have any chance at all, even if they had known CPR. Hana, you did everything perfectly in there. For your first code, you were steady as a rock; but this poor child had no chance."

"So, was it pointless to try to save her?" Hana whimpered.

"Not pointless, Hana. Although we can't perform miracles, we occasionally get to witness miracles, and with young drowning victims, there have been a few miraculous recoveries. We did our best. It's our job to do our best to try to save people, but it's also our job to recognize and accept our limitations."

"I have a three-year-old niece that looks just like her," Hana sobbed. "I can't imagine! My heart is breaking. I'm really sorry, but I don't know if I can do this."

"No problem, Hana. Your shift ends in a few minutes, so just leave as soon as you feel composed enough to transport yourself. I do think you have the steel to be an ER nurse, but you have to give it some thought. An RN is a wonderful degree to have, and you can do lots of different things with it. I'll give you a good recommendation if you want to transfer to another department. Just let me know in advance of your next shift."

Hana sniffled for a minute. She shook the soft brown curls that framed her tear-streaked hollow cheeks. She blew her nose, took a few deep breaths and wiped at her eyes. Finally, she started to nod her head yes and said, "Thanks for your confidence in me, Dr. Volkov. I'll be okay. I promise I'll be here for my next shift. I'm going to go wash my face and I'll be right back to sign my cases over to the nightshift. Thanks for helping me to get through this."

As Dewy watched short stocky Olga and long lean Hana walk down the hall with the physician's arm around the nurse's waist, she pushed the Farrells out of her thoughts. Dewy had sensed she was in the company of a great teacher when she had spent two shifts following the elderly Dr. Olga Volkov around. Now, watching this mentor salvage a young woman's ego and career in such a tragic setting, and in such a kind way, she realized that regardless of specialty, most doctors functioned as psychiatrists.

Dewy started to wonder if the most challenging psychiatric patients might actually be in the ER. In just her initial time there, she'd seen all kinds of craziness. Then she learned that it was the second-year psych resident who got assigned to tell this family that their drowned daughter had died. Bereavement counseling would become her job in her next year of residency. She shuddered at the thought.

Dewy peeked into the code room just as a nurse was making the little body look presentable. She dropped her stethoscope and clasped her hand over her face. The drowned little girl looked like the picture she had seen that morning of Dr. Patel's daughter. She picked up her stethoscope and ran to the area where the families of the critical waited. She gasped with relief when she didn't see Brent Patel there, just other distressed people, some pacing and some looking shell-shocked. Tonight, she was glad she wasn't the psych resident.

When she returned to the clinical area, sign-outs were already in progress. Dr. Brody Jones was covering rooms five to eight. In room five, there was a seventy-year-old retired policemen with chest pain. His primary care physician had recently died, and the man hadn't yet found a new doctor. "Call the cardiology fellow for admission if his enzymes come back elevated," Brody advised.

Dr. Jones walked them into the hall where he explained: "The other guy in this room is a nineteen-year-old overdose. He's a college student home for the summer. His mother thinks his girlfriend broke up with him yesterday, and late this afternoon, she couldn't wake him up. He did wake up in the ambulance and vomited, so we think he's out of the danger zone. His drug screen is still pending. Once he's cleared by psych, he can be discharged."

"Will they admit him if they think he still wants to kill himself?" Dewy asked.

"Good question," Brody said, "but I don't know the answer. Hopefully the psych resident does."

Dewy gulped.

"Room six is a fourteen-year-old skate-boarder who fell backwards on concrete, no helmet. He's cognitively okay now, but his buddy says he was out cold for at least five minutes and confused after that. The neurology resident will see him once his brain MRI gets done.

"Skateboarder's roommate is a sixteen-year-old cyclist who went over the handlebars wearing just shorts and flip-flops. He's got fractures of his jaw, wrists, left knee, and multiple ribs, but his biggest problem is bad road burn. He needs general anesthesia so they can dig all of the gravel out of his face, chest, hands and legs. We started antibiotics and he's on a morphine drip while we wait for an OR. He'll need skin grafts when he gets past this."

"Are you in the surgery program, Dr. Jones?" Dewy asked, studying the smooth skin of his youthful-looking face.

"I'm planning to be a plastic surgeon. Is it that obvious?" Brody observed Dewy's delicate features and thought there wasn't much there for a plastic surgeon to rearrange. She was pretty cute as is.

"Well, you were already planning this poor kid's reconstruction."

"Because he looks like raw hamburger. He will need skin grafts. The attending surgeon wants an hourly blood count to make sure there's no internal bleeding, and we're monitoring his oxygen in case there's a lung contusion. He's had a tetanus shot."

They moved to room seven. "The patient in bed A is two months pregnant and she's had bad morning sickness. Today she threw up a lot and got lightheaded, so her husband brought her in. Her obstetrician said to hydrate and discharge her. In bed B is a thirty-year-old waitress with a history of intractable migraines. She also vomited enough to get dehydrated. Her headache's improving, and she can be discharged when she can hold down some fluids."

As they exited to the hallway and Dewy turned towards room eight, Brody grabbed her hand and pulled her back. "Uh...I've been *un*assigned to room eight today, thankfully. I heard you survived in there last night. Kudos to you! So far, the nurses have been able to handle it since there haven't been any screaming episodes. We're just monitoring the baby's in-and-out fluids. Here comes Hana, her nurse, so she can fill you in on the details.

"I'm outta here. Have a good shift," Brody said, as he strode to the exit.

Hana appeared to have done a good job of pulling herself together. "Hi, Dr. Meadows." The young nurse took in a deep breath before spewing: "I've been in and out of the baby's room all day, so as Dr. Jones just said, I can fill you in on the details, tell you what's going on, make sure you've got the big picture, help you see past everyone else's biases, try not to agitate the baby when you change the bag, be really careful not to spill it, don't come in here with blood on your scrubs, you need to upgrade this call button system, clean your stethoscope, wash your hands, turn the lights down, turn the a/c up, turn it off if you can't make it quieter."

Hana caught her breath, shook her head and looked like she might cry again.

"I know, Hana. I know. It's unbearable," Dewy commiserated. "Just a minute in that room makes you feel like you're a punching bag. It's such an uncomfortable vibe that it makes me wonder if that's what makes the baby scream. Can you imagine being one of her kids? I feel like screaming myself when I'm in there.

"You hang in there, Hana. These people will soon be gone. Experience like this will make us better professionals and stronger people. You've had a wicked day, Hana. Go treat yourself to something special. Just tell me if you observed anything that might help us understand what could be going on with this baby."

"Well, just once when I was in there, the baby was in a recliner, sucking on a rattle, and she suddenly got this pained look on her face. She also started to sweat, and her heart rate went up. She didn't cry vocally. Carol was on the phone at the time, so I tried to amuse Darryl, but she met my smile with a grimace. It only lasted for maybe a minute, but it definitely looked like something was hurting her.

"For a second, I thought she could be having a seizure, but I don't really think that was it. I don't know. I have a cousin who's my age and when she was seven, she got diagnosed with a kind of epilepsy called absence seizures. Her only symptom was that she often didn't know what someone had just said to her. Ever since she's been on seizure medicine, she can follow a conversation and she's fine."

"Thanks, Hana. That's a really good idea. Anything else you observed?"

"Hmm, later in the afternoon Darryl did cry, but her mother said it was her hunger cry, and not her pain cry. Carol was very emphatic about that. Darryl stopped crying as soon as I gave her a pacifier. I did get reprimanded that it was cruel to keep a baby hungry in order to rest her stomach. That's all I can tell you. I hope you can have a good shift."

Chapter Ten

After rounding on the signed-over patients along with nurse Gus, Dr. Dewy Meadows was impressed with Dr. Brody Jones. He seemed to have everything under control. Dewy took care of a new patient with an ankle sprain, and finally, she gathered the courage to enter room eight.

"It's about time," Carol greeted her. "There hasn't been a goddamn doctor in here all day since that jerk Dr. Jones was in here this morning. He did absolutely nothing and I'll bet I get a bill for physician services anyway.

"This evening, I went to the cafeteria for only fifteen minutes, and when I came back, Darryl's pee bag was almost overflowing. It took another ten minutes to get anyone's attention. If that bag had leaked, the whole goddamn test would be no good and I'd still get the bill.

"I've been reading about this tumor on Google. It's a nightmare. You know how much this stupid test must be costing my insurance company? It's a ridiculously expensive test. This whole thing is ridiculous."

"But we're almost there, Mrs. Farrell. In just ninety minutes we'll have our twenty-four-hour specimen and you can get out of here. And maybe we'll have an answer and we'll be able to help your baby."

"Yeah, by cutting her open and looking for a few cells in her adrenal gland; like looking for a needle in a haystack. I read about it. It's a horror show."

"It is, Mrs. Farrell. I don't know what's worse; finding that she has the tumor or telling you we don't know what's wrong. Both options are terrible, except one presents the possibility of a cure."

Just as Dewy ran out of arguments, Darryl started to cry. "That's her hunger cry. You bastards haven't let her eat for a whole day and I know from experience that IV fluids don't satisfy hunger. They just make you pee a lot. Now are you going to let this poor hungry baby eat or not? I need a bottle of her special formula, which I'll bet we have to wait an hour for your stupid pharmacy to send over."

"I agree. Let's feed her so we can observe her while she eats. Her nurse said she had no screaming episodes since that one this morning. Is that an improvement over recent days?"

"Hard to know in just one day. She probably screams with feedings one out of three times, and there have been days without screaming episodes. I don't know anymore and neither do any of you damn doctors. All you idiot doctors can do is run expensive tests that don't show anything. I'm sick of this. My whole family is stressed out because of this."

Darryl's crying intensified. "She needs to eat. She's on Good Start and one of your staff better go get her that formula right now. You'll probably find it in the neonatal unit, because they give it to the preemies. And if you can't get her the damn formula, at least give her some sugar water. Sometimes, the sugar makes her stop crying, but sometimes she screams and won't take it."

"Let me get on that right now, Mrs. Farrell. It's really important that we get to see what happens when we go from resting her stomach to feeding her, so I'm with you on not letting her be hungry. I'll be back as soon as I can get her something."

Dewy raced out of the room, but had to pause after closing the door behind her to tell herself to relax, or as her brain dictated in Russian, *rass-la-bit'sya,*

Gus used his charm to wrangle a bottle of the formula from a neonatal nurse, and then he and Dewy watched as Darryl eagerly wolfed it down. She almost drained the bottle, but then she abruptly stopped and started to wail. It was pitiful! She screamed for five minutes and then Carol started screaming along with her. "This is what happens. This happens multiple times a day. Someone has to stop this! This is intolerable! I can't take this anymore! Please, do something! Please, help my baby!"

Gus gently rubbed Darryl's abdomen, but she continued to scream. Dewy tried to put a hand on Carol's shoulder and got pushed away. She felt utterly helpless and stood there frozen, just watching the heart rate monitor jump around until the screaming finally stopped.

Carol waited a few seconds before offering the bottle again, and Darryl eagerly resumed feeding and finished her meal. Then she promptly filled her diaper and Gus took on that project, while Dewy approached Carol.

"I'm so sorry I don't have an answer for your baby, Mrs. Farrell, but watching her go through that just now, I can't help but wonder if there's something in her stomach that's blocking the flow of formula. Is it possible she swallowed something that one of the other kids gave her?"

"They looked for that already. They took x-rays and did an ultrasound and they didn't see a damn thing. Then they wanted to scope her and look in there. So, I let them do that and they didn't find a damn thing. Poor baby had to have an empty stomach and anesthesia and the tests were of no help at all."

"When did they do that?" Dewy wondered if Carol was frustrated enough to start to reveal her other medical encounters.

"A few weeks ago, at Pine Meadow Medical Center. Then, they said they wanted to have her swallow barium and take more x-rays of her stomach. She's already had enough radiation to kill an elephant. There's an old doctor there who knew of a rare case of a baby who had an extra stomach attached to their stomach, like a side pouch. The little stomach would fill up and cause pain until the milk would overflow into the bigger stomach and go down into the intestines. They could only see the little stomach when they put the barium in there and took more x-rays. So, I let them do that and guess what? She only has one stomach.

"Let's just fry my baby with x-rays. I took her to a chiropractor that specializes in babies last month, and she took spinal x-rays and she didn't find anything wrong, and my insurance company won't pay for that, so I have to.

"Last month, the doctors at University ER sedated her to check her eyes and that was also normal. How many times are you damn doctors going to radiate this baby and put her under anesthesia?"

"That really is concerning, Mrs. Farrell, I agree. Babies this young are extra sensitive to radiation and anesthetics. Have there been other occasions where they took x-rays or sedated her? Maybe they didn't appreciate how much radiation she was getting." Dewy picked at the corners of the consent forms on her clipboard. "Who's managing her formula changes?"

"I've been working with the nurse-practitioner at the Oak Street Clinic, a so-called colic expert. When I was breast-feeding, the expert just kept changing my diet. Then I gave up breast-feeding because Darryl started to do this thing where she'd latch on, suckle, then cry, then do it again and again. She wasn't gaining weight and my nipples were so sore I needed pain medicine, so we put Darryl on formula.

"She seems to scream less with bottle-feeding and her weight caught up, but for the last month, the screaming has been getting gradually more frequent and more intense. In the past five weeks, she's been on three different formulas and the screaming just gets worse. It's terrorizing my other kids. Someone needs to do something."

"Mrs. Farrell, do you think Darryl might ever have seizures, like maybe she trembles, or foams at the mouth, or stares off into space, or seems like she's lost touch with her surroundings? Have you ever noticed anything like that?"

For a minute, Carol was speechless. She seemed to really be thinking about it.

"Have any of the doctors she's seen checked her for seizures?" Dewy asked.

"The pediatrician I was going to asked me if there was any history of seizures in the family. I told him we don't know my husband's family history. My husband was a dirty little toddler in diapers when he was found wandering along a highway. His adoptive mother told me that the only thing he could tell anyone was that his name was Harold and he held up three fingers if asked his age. He didn't really start to talk until he was about five.

"There are no seizures in my family that I know of, although I have a cat who has seizures. Do you think that's what it could be? How can we check for that? That idiot pediatrician never suggested we check for seizures. He said it was colic. He was too busy, and I stopped going there."

"Subtle seizures can be detected by measuring electrical impulses given off by the brain through the skull. It's called EEG, *electro-encephalo-gram*. They tape some wires to the scalp and watch the flow of electrical current from different parts of the brain. It's painless and there's no radiation. I'm going to go try to arrange an EEG for Darryl. And look, it's quarter past nine. Our test time is over. I'm going to send Gus back in here to get the last of the urine while I get that consult set up."

"Mrs. Farrell, it would really help if you'd sign these forms so we can get the records of the other tests that Darryl has already had. We'd like to avoid any unnecessary radiation or medication. It's your choice of course." Dewy handed the clipboard to Carol and escaped before she could throw it back at her.

"But this *is* an emergency," Dewy pleaded with the neurology resident on call, who replied that there were no openings on the EEG lab schedule for two weeks.

"I really can't make an exception for a crying baby who has no history of head trauma or other risk factors," the resident declared.

"If you heard her cry, you would," Dewy argued.

The neurology resident said, "sorry, no can do."

Dewy went back into room eight. "Okay, Mrs. Farrell, I need your help. The next time Darryl has a screaming fit; I need you to film it. Can you do that on your phone? I think seeing what you're dealing with is the best way for me to get Darryl on the EEG schedule quickly. When you've done that, send it to me through the patient portal." Dewy wrote down some information and handed it to Carol, who had set the clipboard down without signing the consent forms. Dewy took the clipboard back and left the forms with Carol.

"You'll get a text as soon as the scheduler can set up an EEG appointment, and the results of the urine test can be viewed online through the patient portal. Gus will get you signed out. Get me that video and I'll do everything in my power to help you."

Dewy bolted out the door before Carol could say a word. She was pleasantly surprised when Gus came out of the room a little later with some signed consent forms.

Chapter Eleven

*D*ewy scheduled an appointment with the psychiatry department chairman on her day off. She waited outside Dr. Ortiz's office for a long time and when she finally got brought back, Dr. Ortiz was on the phone for another five minutes, arguing with someone about cuts to research funding. Finally, she slammed the phone down and turned her attention to Dewy.

"Sorry about that, Dr. Meadows. This morning I was notified that our research funding is being pared down about ten percent, and what to cut will be a truly despicable decision. However, I promise you I won't cut funding from the linguistics research. Your video showing how differently people react to differently worded questions about the same thing was just brilliant. I'd love to talk to you about it, but you came to see me about the Farrells."

Dr. Linda Ortiz's shaking head seemed to say, "I know how crazy they are."

Dewy gave a brief summary of the baby's presentation, what she had learned about the tragic case of Merrill's gallbladder parasite, and her frustration with trying to interact with Carol. "Is there anything you can tell me about this family that will help me to follow up with them when we get the test results back? Dr. Patel said you know them well."

"Dr. Patel has been worried about the Farrell kids for years. He's especially concerned about Merrill. That kid has had a lot more than his fair share of misfortune.

"I read your ER notes, Dewy. There is such a thing as 'screaming seizures' where the only symptom is unprovoked screaming. It was a good idea to send the baby for EEG. I'm truly impressed that you've gained Carol's cooperation.

"As you've already heard, Merrill's case was a disaster. There are almost no reports of giardia in the gallbladders of children, and few reports of it in adults, so it just wasn't something most doctors would even think to look for. Carol has justification for being furious with the health care system in general, but her personality disorders cause her to project that anger onto the providers that are trying to help her."

"Did you say disorders plural?" Dewy asked. "I thought her obsessive-compulsive disorder was classic."

"It's textbook classic, Dewy, but Carol is a whole lot more than OCD. As you'll learn from your patients, people who others dislike often suffer from a hodgepodge of personality disorders. Many also have mood disorders. Counting her OCD, Carol presents with a few features of maybe six of the ten common personality disorders: narcissistic, paranoid, histrionic, borderline, and most obviously, schizotypal personality disorder."

"Um, I'm not remembering the main features of schizotypal," Dewy admitted.

"People with schizotypal disorder are eccentric. They're odd-balls. They rarely if ever form close relationships. They don't understand relationships, and they don't perceive the impact of their behavior on others. It differs from schizoid personality disorder in that schizoid people avoid social interaction altogether, and rarely show emotion if they do interact. They are the lone wolves of the world. Schizotypal people aren't avoidant of social contact; they're just bad at it. I wish they'd change the name 'schizotypal.' It makes no sense and it's confusing.

"There is some interesting new research that shows how the brains of people with borderline personality disorder process social information. The researchers watched people's brain activity on a PET scanner while the subjects looked at pictures of faces. Healthy subjects showed activity in certain areas of their brain when they looked at happy faces, and their brains lit up in other areas if the picture showed an angry or a sad face.

"When borderline subjects looked at the same pictures, their brains reacted to neutral facial expressions as if the pictures showed hostility. These poor people must walk around thinking that everyone is frowning at them. No wonder they're insecure and distrusting. We're starting to understand that personality disorders are really brain disorders.

"In addition to her personality disorders, Carol's behavior is largely controlled by a faulty circuit that turns her every thought into a vocalization. If she thinks it, she says it. She can't hold it back. For her, it's like a maddening itch that doesn't get scratched unless she verbalizes whatever pops into her head, and she has no idea how to modulate her voice. I don't believe she can help it. I'll bet if Carol's in a pleasant situation, she narrates how blue the sky is and how pretty the lighting is, how nice the breeze is and how perfect the temperature is. The problem for us is that we only see Carol when she's in a terrible situation, when her children are suffering and we're unable to help.

"Carol's also a domineering personality, not one of the main recognized disorders, but I think it should be. I also think her high energy level borders on mania, and I wonder if she also has bouts of depression. She does have superior intellect, but as is true with most personality disordered patients, she lacks insight."

"So, what's her relationship with her husband like?" Dewy asked.

"That's a whole other story, Dewy. When we had multiple doctors trying to figure out why Merrill had bellyaches, I interviewed Carol by herself, Harold by himself, and then the two of them together. I also interviewed Carol's mother because she was present during Merrill's disastrous hospitalization. She's an interesting lady too, except that she's totally sane. She's a semi-retired math professor, recently married to an economics professor, and she gave me some background about her struggle to raise Carol, as well as information about Harold. She also appears to be a very dedicated grandmother to Carol's kids.

"Carol's mother, Molly Hudson, told me that Carol may have suffered head trauma when she was four. Molly went to pick her up at nursery school and was told that Carol had been crying on the playground, and another child said the swing hit her in the head. They didn't find any bumps on her head and she stopped crying and wanted to go back to playing, so they thought she was okay. But an hour later she got whiney and said her head hurt, so they called Molly to come get her.

"Molly's pediatrician diagnosed a concussion and said to take Carol to the ER if she vomited or got worse. Initially, she seemed okay, but gradually over a few weeks, Molly perceived that Carol wasn't the same little girl she had been. She became irritable and she incessantly prattled and griped about everything. Molly took her to a pediatric neurologist who said her exam, imaging, and labs were all fine. A pediatric psychiatrist had nothing to offer.

"Molly was convinced that the head trauma was the cause of her daughter's problems until a generation later when Gerald came along. Molly started to see some of Carol's personality traits showing up in Gerald when he was four. The similarities were remarkable enough that Molly concluded that Carol's quirks weren't caused by trauma but were genetic. She described Carol's biologic father as an excessively talkative guy with a sour disposition. He was a philosophy professor. They divorced when Carol was eight, and Carol has no relationship with her father or with her older sister.

"Then there's Harold, a classic Asperger's Syndrome; but having worked with so many fascinating Asperger's people, 'classic' is a bad choice of words. They're all uniquely interesting. Harold's about six or seven years older than Carol, early forties, I think. He was an abandoned child raised by a loving adoptive family, but he doesn't seem to have much of a relationship with them, or anybody else except Carol and the kids, and he seems to relate to the kids on a childlike level.

"No one has ever uncovered the story of how he came to be abandoned. He doesn't remember anything about his early life, and he's not interested in doing a genetic search to find biologic relatives. He's bright, but he said he couldn't really master reading until he was sixteen. He always liked to draw exploded diagrams of things and make models.

"When Harold was fourteen, he got hit in the face with a tennis racket and lost his two front teeth. When the dentist glued in replacements, they looked too big, like horse teeth, and he was nicknamed 'Horseface.' After that, Harold became interested in creating pretty teeth. Last I heard, he was operating a dental lab that employs multiple technicians who carve out prosthetic teeth for the patients of a hundred or so area dentists. And Harold still likes to make teeth himself, or at least he likes to be in the lab all day. Carol does all of his accounting, and she also seems to be a very savvy investor. They're definitely not hurting for money.

"When I tried to interview them together during Merrill's illness, Carol did one hundred percent of the talking. Harold just sat there ogling her. He gets this look on his face like he can't believe he's with this beautiful woman, and he can't really focus on a word she says. He smiles a lot, and nods when Carol prods him. They say, 'there's a lid for every pot' and for all practical purposes, Carol and Harold Farrell were made for each other; they're the perfect couple. I don't know if that helps you any, Dewy, but that's my read on this very challenging family."

"What do you think drives Carol to keep having babies? Dewy asked. "It seems like she takes care of them, but it's not in an affectionate way, like she's not really attached to them. I don't know how to explain it."

"I believe that's an accurate observation, Dewy, and a very good question. Maybe she has the kids because she can control them. Her oldest, a very passive daughter, follows her commands exactly like Harold does.

"Maybe it's because no one in the world other than family will have anything to do with her. Maybe it's because she turned Harold into the greatest lover in the world by giving him crystal clear instructions, and the man apparently does have skillful hands. Maybe he can actually please this woman. Maybe Carol's schizotypal disorder enables her to believe she has good relationships with her children.

"I don't really know, but I think it's possible that for Carol, they're a collection. For some people it's coins or stamps and for some its cars. I once had a patient who had two thousand poodle figurines. For Carol, it seems to be cats and kids. I think she loves them as possessions. There's a fine line between collectors and hoarders, but one of the differences is that collectors take care of their collections. Carol takes care of her cats and her kids. Now we have to hope we can take care of this baby, if she allows us to do so."

"Thank you, Dr. Ortiz for your time and insight. I think that does help me. This family's an unbelievable teaching case, and *muchas gracias* for supporting my linguistics research. I sure wish you luck with your budget dilemma and hope I can make your research program shine."

Chapter Twelve

*D*ewy was back on the dayshift. At seven a.m. the ER was eerily quiet, like the calm before the storm. As she waited for Dr. Brody Jones to finish up with a laceration so he could sign over his patients, Xray handed her two discs from Community General Hospital, a disc from University Hospital, and a paper record from a pediatrician, all regarding Darryl Farrell.

Dewy popped one of the discs into a computer and saw numerous pages, all looking like cookie cutter copies of the others. It would take hours to find the sprinkling of word changes, if there were any. The other disc contained imaging studies. She'd need to consult with a radiologist and get all of the records scanned into the system.

As she watched Xray attend to a screen full of cardiac monitors, Dr. Brody Jones appeared. "Dr. Meadows, how nice to see you fresh-faced at the beginning of a shift, instead of droopy eyed at the end. I just stayed late to do a two-layer closure on the leg of a chef who dropped a meat cleaver on himself. I wrote the discharge order, but you might want to take a look, in case you're here when he comes back for a recheck. It came together really well.

"I had a great night," Brody boasted. "Dr. Olga hates to sew and so does the senior resident, so Liselle triaged all of the lacerations to me, and I spent the shift in the suture room and got a lot of experience. I saw a bunch of kitchen workers with cuts and burns.

"I only have two beds to sign out to you. In room seven, there's a fifty-year-old alcoholic diabetic with an infected leg ulcer down to the bone. He could lose the leg. Internal medicine and surgery are debating about whose service to admit him to, so you just have to keep his antibiotics going until someone finds him a bed.

"Did you know room eight is a soundproof room with a video camera? I didn't know until last night. Anyway, the patient in there is a nursing home resident with dementia. He's eighty-one. He reportedly climbed over his bed guardrail and fell and broke his hip. He's since been trying to walk around on an unstable femur.

"Warning: he spits, hits and bites, but he's no threat, now that he's sedated. I can't fathom how the nursing home staff manages him. Last night, he punched the admitting nurse hard enough to bruise her chin. Ortho will take him to pin the hip when an OR opens."

Dewy found herself looking for stubble on Brody's youthful face. Maybe there was peach fuzz on his chin, but she couldn't even see hair follicles on his exceptionally smooth and rosy skin. He had ample strawberry blond hair with robust eyebrows, so it wasn't alopecia. His voice was deep, and he seemed to have way too much swagger to be testosterone deficient. She guessed he was just one of those men who was genetically beardless.

"Well thanks for staying late and doing the lac." Dewy said. "Sewing isn't my favorite thing either."

Their conversation abruptly ended when Xray appeared and said he needed her in the ambulance foyer. She was ready to run, but X said, "no hurry. They just need an MD to document dead on arrival, so the ER doesn't have to admit him. He probably died just before the ambulance got here."

After that, Dewy saw a variety of common illnesses and injuries and a teenager who had badly burned his scalp with some kind of homemade hair dye. Just when it seemed like her shift might be easy, Xray intercepted her in the hallway. "I've got a special surprise for you, Dr. Meadows; someone whose language you speak, but it's not a foreign language."

Dewy furrowed her brow in puzzlement.

"It's Gerald Farrell. He's here with his grandmother for fever and maybe an infected bug bite." Xray handed her the chart.

"As in one of Carol Farrell's kids?" Dewy fretted. "Is his mother here?"

"Relax! Grandma Molly says Carol's home with the baby. I think it was Carol who called a little while ago and asked if you're here today. Gerald's temperature is a one-o-two though they gave him Tylenol an hour ago. Grandma Molly says none of the other kids have been sick. You can stop sweating, Dewy. Grandma Molly is as nice as Carol is nasty."

Grandma Molly Hudson looked like an older version of her daughter. She had the same pale blue eyes, Cupid's bow lips, and angelic face as Carol, though she was a bit taller and thinner than her daughter, and her hair was silver. Gerald also looked like Carol and had her fair coloring, the striking blue eyes and honey-colored hair. He was sitting in his grandmother's lap and rubbing his knees. Dewy introduced herself and asked how she could help.

Grandma Molly held out Gerald's left forearm where Dewy observed inflamed scratched skin. "Last Thursday," Molly began, "he came home from camp with quite a few bug bites, even though we slather him with repellant. This child is a mosquito magnet.

"On Friday, this bite looked infected, so his mom took him to an urgent care clinic, and they put him on an antibiotic. Now the bite looks much better, but Gerald isn't acting like himself. He's normally a very active child and since the weekend, he's been mopey and sleepy. It's unusual for him to nap and he's also lost his appetite.

Carol's kept him home from camp the past two days, and he's been complaining of headaches and his knees hurting. Today we noticed he has fever and he's extra grumpy.

"Carol thinks you're a good, caring physician, Dr. Meadows, and coming from her, that's quite a compliment."

With Gerald sitting restlessly in Molly's lap, Dewy noted his throat to be red and his eyes looked bloodshot. The knees didn't seem hot or swollen. "Let's lie you down on the table, Gerald, so I can check your tummy." Dewy went to pick him up and he let out a holler when she put her hands under his arms. "What hurts Gerald?"

Gerald put his right hand in his left armpit and said "ow."

Dewy took off his t-shirt, lifted his arms up and noticed a prominent swelling in his left armpit. As she attempted to feel it, Gerald cried out. She then found some swollen glands in his neck, also quite tender. When she examined his abdomen, he complained of pain when she tried to feel his spleen. She did a skin survey and noted bug bites and scratches all over his arms and legs. "Did one of the kitties scratch you, Gerald?"

"Bluto did it. He's a bad kitty. So is Bingo. I hate Bingo."

"When did Bluto scratch you, Gerald? Did you tell Mommy that Bluto scratched you?" Molly asked her grandson.

"Bluto always scratches me, and he hisses at me. I hate Bluto and I hate Bingo. Bingo's a stupid cat. She runs away from me and she sleeps on top of Mommy's van."

Dewy and Molly exchanged sideways glances and Dewy told them she'd be right back. She quickly reviewed cat scratch disease and realized that its symptoms could be due to a variety of illnesses ranging from common strep throat to tuberculosis, cancer or AIDS. Poor little Gerald was going to need some tests to sort it out. She explained to Molly that they needed to draw blood and do a TB test.

Dewy managed to catch Dr. Patel between patients and she told him about Gerald.

"Interesting," he said. "We usually see cat-scratch disease in the fall or winter, but with that house full of cats, it's amazing the whole family's not in here with it all year. Let's just hope this little guy doesn't have lymphoma. With all the cats and bug bites, you also need to consider other diseases caused by mosquitos, fleas and ticks."

"Do you think we need to biopsy the big lymph node?" Dewy asked.

"Let's hope not. It's good that the nodes are tender because with lymphoma, which is not uncommon in kids, the swollen glands don't usually hurt. See what his labs show. Of all the things that make lymph nodes blow up, cat scratch fever could be the best diagnosis, though for patients, it's as nasty as mono. We can't cure mononucleosis or cat scratch fever, but after a couple of months of patient misery, these illnesses go away on their own."

Dr. Patel patted Dewy's shoulder and ran off to take care of an actively seizing ten-year-old who'd been hit in the head with a baseball bat.

Gerald's blood cell counts came back a little low, and he had a high 'sed rate' indicating serious inflammation. The test didn't identify what was inflamed, but the higher the sed rate, the more serious the problem. Gerald's sed rate was high enough to be worrisome. It would need to be followed.

Dewy explained to Molly that they suspected that Gerald had cat scratch disease, but they couldn't be sure until test results came back, which was going to take a few days. He'd also need to return in two to three days for the nurse to read the TB test. There was no known cure for cat scratch disease and they'd just have to manage the symptoms.

Molly asked some appropriate questions and when it appeared that she was ready to leave, Dewy reluctantly asked her how the baby was doing.

"She's getting worse," Molly answered. "She goes for her EEG this afternoon. That's why I'm here with Gerald. Carol didn't want to get stuck here and miss that appointment. I really appreciate that you're trying to help us with Darryl, Dr. Meadows. We're at our wits' end with that poor baby."

"I know," Dewy said. "I hope we can find some easy answers for both of your grandkids. I'm so sorry the baby is still crying. Maybe the EEG will solve this mystery."

A few hours later, Dewy got a call from the technician in the EEG lab, telling her that Darryl needed to be rescheduled. The baby had slept through the whole study and they wanted to repeat the test when she was having one of her screaming fits.

After some heated back and forth, Carol agreed to bring the baby to do it again when the technician made special accommodations. They had no openings on the schedule for weeks, but the situation prompted the technician to do the test on her own time early the next morning when the baby was being fed, because that was when she was most likely to scream.

Dewy thanked the technician for her extra effort.

"I just had to do it," the woman said. "When my son was failing second grade, it took more than a dozen doctor appointments before they figured out that he was having micro-seizures. Once he got on seizure medicine, he became a good student. That's when I went to school to learn how to do EEGs.

"I can really empathize with this mother, especially after seeing the video of that poor baby screaming like that. It was actually upsetting to watch."

Chapter Thirteen

*D*ewy Meadows was exhausted when her shift ended, but she was still preoccupied with the Farrells. Worrying about the baby helped distract her from worrying about why her boyfriend Alex wasn't answering her calls, texts or E-mails. He was a truly considerate person, so his ignoring her communication didn't make sense, and she was starting to worry that something terrible had happened to him.

She tried to call the hospital where he was doing his residency, but they wouldn't give her any information due to privacy rules. She'd also called his father, but he also hadn't returned her calls. Dewy was as distressed about it as she was exhausted. She felt a little revived after grabbing some dinner in the hospital cafeteria, and she went from there to the records room to look at Darryl's discs.

The records from Community General showed that on her first visit, Darryl was crying so frantically they couldn't examine her. Carol had some of her younger kids with her, and the physician noted that the little boy was hyperactive. At one point, he picked up a younger sister, swung her around and dropped her on the floor. The doctor then wondered if this child, or any of the kids might have done something to the baby when Carol wasn't looking. He sedated the infant and had her entire skeleton x-rayed, but there were no fractures.

On her second visit to that ER, Darryl arrived crying, but by the time she was seen by a physician, she was fast asleep. Her exam and labs were all normal. It was suggested that Carol consult with a family counselor to help her deal with the tension being caused by the colic. The mere suggestion of a counseling consult sent Carol into a rage. She stormed out of the hospital, threatening to sue them for not doing anything to help the baby.

The disc from University Hospital showed a single ER visit for screaming. That episode started when Carol was walking Darryl in her stroller. It was a windy day and maybe, something blew in her eye. Being familiar with the Farrells from prior encounters, and knowing the infamous story of Merrill's gallbladder parasite, the ER doctor brought in an ophthalmologist to check Darryl's eyes, not only for corneal trauma, but for disease inside the eye caused by a cat-associated parasite called *toxo-plas-mosis.*

Dewy learned that the toxoplasmosis parasite often lives in healthy cats and their humans without causing symptoms. However, if a pregnant mother who harbors the parasite transmits it to her fetus, the fetus who survives pregnancy can have severe problems, including seizures and blindness. Fortunately, baby Darryl's corneas and retinas looked healthy.

The printouts of the pediatrician's notes were just a lot of computer puke. The only thing different from visit to visit was the date, the growth measurements, and the vaccine record. Every visit note began with:

This is a well-nourished, well-developed female infant here for a well-baby check. The mother reports excessive crying.

Then the notes described perfect body parts in textbook lingo for every exam.

As a medical student, Dewy had learned that the only way to expediently get visits written up in a complex computer program was to click through a template. Trying to thoughtfully describe the patient took time you didn't have. It was a sham, but it was the way of computerized health care.

Along with the bogus doctor notes from the pediatrician's office, there were also notes from a nurse practitioner who managed breast-feeding and colic. These notes were also useless templates, and Dewy was about to forgo looking at the back pages, when she noticed that the print on those pages appeared to have come from a different computer.

Those pages turned out to be Darryl's birth records from Pine Meadow Medical Center. Dewy read an admitting note that a caring nurse-midwife had bothered to type up.

This 35-year-old presented in labor with contractions every 5 minutes. She's had 9 pregnancies, 6 live births, one miscarriage and one still-born. Her living children are 14, 12, 10, 7, 6 and 4 years old. Her 2nd child, Terrell, was born 3 weeks prematurely and did well. Third child, Merrill, was born 10 weeks prematurely and had a protracted course in the neonatal intensive care unit. Merrill has asthma but the other kids are reportedly healthy.

Carol had a first trimester miscarriage between Merrill and her 4th child, Gerald.

In her 8th pregnancy 2 years ago, Carol tested positive for toxoplasmosis. She had no symptoms and her amniotic fluid tested negative for the parasite. However, fetal ultrasound at 15 weeks showed that the fetus had an abnormally small brain and an enlarged liver. A week later, Carol spontaneously aborted a stillborn fetus with features of congenital toxoplasmosis.

Carol demanded that she be treated for toxoplasmosis before she started this pregnancy. She did a 4-week course of multiple anti-parasitic

medicines. She was also informed that with cats in the home, there was
no guarantee that she would remain free of the parasite, and she was
warned against attending to the cats' litter boxes.

Dewy skipped to the summary on the last page of the birth records.

Carol's labor progressed without problems and she delivered a healthy,
full-term, eight-pound baby girl who breastfed well. The Farrells were
discharged to follow-up with their pediatrician.

Dewy was suddenly struck by the recollection that Carol had mentioned having Darryl seen at Pine Meadow Medical Center where they scoped her GI tract and did a barium swallow, but Carol hadn't included Pine Meadow on the consent forms. Maybe she didn't know that the birth records from that hospital were part of the pediatrician's chart. Maybe her defensiveness about the cats was motivating her to want to conceal the information about toxoplasmosis, but why? Everyone seemed to already know about her cat addiction because of Merrill's gallbladder infection.

Had Dewy known about the history of toxoplasmosis, she would have tested Gerald for that too. After reading more about this parasite, she realized it was only dangerous to fetuses and people with immune deficiency. According to Grandma Molly, Gerald was a healthy kid, but was he? As Dewy walked to her apartment, she wondered what else was going on with this family that Carol didn't want to reveal.

Still preoccupied with the Farrells when she got home, she tried to read some more about infections contracted from bug bites. She got through Lyme disease, dengue fever, yellow fever, and eastern equine encephalitis, but in the middle of west Nile virus, she fell into a deep sleep, a well-deserved *schlafen*, as her German-speaking father used to say.

Chapter Fourteen

Under an ominous looking sky, Dewy walked to the ER to start her dayshift. Static electricity in the air made her spine tingle. The forecast was for torrential rain with gale force winds. The TV weatherwoman had commented about dangerous storms becoming more frequent and outpacing the capacity of first responders. Drivers were urged to use extra caution.

Upon arrival, Dewy had no new patients, and Dr. Brody Jones had all of his patients stabilized when he signed them over. He was enviably efficient. The quiet lasted for almost an hour and Dewy spent the time reading more about infectious diseases. Illness caused by parasites was a specialty unto itself.

Her reading time abruptly ended when a procession of ambulances started to arrive bearing bus crash victims. All of the patients were children aged nine and ten, except for two camp counselors and the bus driver who were college students. The bus driver and one of the counselors were unconscious. The other counselor had a broken arm, a concussion and a bleeding scalp, but enough presence of mind to explain what happened.

The minibus was going slowly in the heavy rain. A pickup truck coming from the opposite direction spun out on a curve, and slammed into the side of the bus, which was taking sixteen kids to an indoor skating rink because their outdoor track meet had been rained out. The bus was pushed off the road and down a steep embankment. It landed on its side in a ravine. The counselor was certain that had the bus not been going so slowly, there would have been corpses instead of injured kids.

The rescue workers had to work in crouched or kneeling positions in order to attend to the injured inside the bus. Each of the victims that needed to be on a stretcher had to then be carried up the steep, muddy embankment to where the ambulances were lining up on the closed road. Seven of the children and two of the adults were on backboards and in neck braces. Some of the less injured children were brought to the hospital in police cars.

All of the victims were wet, while the rescue workers were drenched and caked in mud. One of the volunteer ambulance attendants had twisted her ankle slipping down the embankment and it was seriously swollen. A fire department paramedic smashed his elbow on a rock when he fell in the mud. Another rescuer who had gone up and down the embankment multiple times, complained of acute back pain.

"Why aren't they distributing these ambulances to other hospitals?" Dr. Patel asked Xray, who was manning the triage desk.

"I called Central Dispatch about that," X said. "There are accidents on all of the highways and power lines down on the side streets. The whole city's gridlocked with closed roads. We just happen to be the shortest distance from the crash, and the most accessible."

The ER put out a text for help to its roster of off-duty nurses and doctors, and some who lived nearby managed to get there. A neurosurgeon came to help with brain and spine injuries. An ophthalmology resident was attending to a girl with a fractured eye socket. Dewy was impressed when droopy eyed Brody Jones returned to the ER, after having just barely left. "I wasn't really sleepy," he said, "and I didn't want to miss the experience."

"Please be sure you're not too tired," Dewy cautioned.

Brody laughed. "So listen! When my dad trained to be a doctor in the 1980s, he was expected to take care of patients for thirty-six hours straight, three times a week, for four freaking years. So, eighteen hours this one time is no biggie."

Brody assessed a nasty laceration on a child's face. Her forehead and her nose were split open. It was so bad that Brody chose to refer the case to the plastic surgeon on call. This pretty little girl could be badly scarred, and Brody thought she needed more expertise than he could provide. He moved on to a dirty leg laceration on one of the rescue workers.

Dr. Stone was managing a skinny boy with broken ribs and a ruptured spleen. He seemed to be losing blood quickly, and he'd be going to an OR as soon as his blood was typed and cross-matched. Dr. Patel was stabilizing a child with a collapsed lung who was going to be admitted to the intensive care unit.

A community orthopedist showed up. He had privileges in every hospital in the city and a reputation as an ambulance-chaser. On this occasion, he was a welcome staff addition. There were a lot of broken bones. One child had two broken wrists, another had arm bones protruding through the skin. Many needed imaging to rule out pelvic and rib fractures. The bus driver had a smashed jaw.

Dewy was attending to one of the rescue workers in the hallway. She shuddered when she heard someone say, "Keep the ice-pack on your mouth, Merrill." She turned around and followed the wheelchair down the hall until she was able to get a look at the name on the child's wristband. It said Merrill Ray, and this poor little Merrill had a badly injured face and he was spitting up blood. Dewy breathed a sigh of relief that it wasn't one of the Farrell kids, and she went back to evaluating the rescue worker with shoulder pain.

As news of the bus crash got around, distressed parents and some reporters started to show up. Shortly thereafter, the overwrought camp director arrived with the contact information for the parents of the children believed to be on the bus. One of the nurses volunteered to help him call the families, while the reporters flashed cameras in his face and some of the parents berated him. The father of one of the children was apparently an ambulance-chasing attorney. Dr. Patel called the hospital lawyer to come to the ER and persuade the man to stop soliciting clients, and to validate the paperwork that enabled the camp director to give permission to treat the children.

Sometime later, Dewy was counseling the parents of a child with a concussion when she heard a loud familiar voice in the hallway. She felt a chill when she recognized it as belonging to Carol Farrell. As it turned out, the child she had seen spitting up blood was Merrill Ray Farrell. The clerk who had typed up his ID bracelet had only heard him say his first and middle name as he sputtered through his split lips and broken front teeth.

The coward in Dewy wanted to hide somewhere, but she somehow mustered up the courage she needed to try to help this family. She thought there might be something psychiatric going on, and she wanted to be the one to solve this medical mystery and help that poor infant. She finished up with the family she was counseling and went to face the Farrells.

Merrill was one of the less severely injured. He had hit his mouth on the seatback in front of him, and then he toppled sideways and landed on the child who sat in the window seat. The child who fell on top of Merrill was a lightweight, while the child in the window seat sustained a dislocated shoulder and a fractured pelvis. Merrill's other injuries seemed limited to bruises, but he had to be sedated for Brody to repair his lacerated lips.

By the time Carol got news of the accident and arrived in the ER, Merrill was awake but groggy. When Dewy approached her, she was on her phone, frantically trying to find out from the camp where her other kids were. Her daughter Cheryl was holding Baby Darryl. The infant sat quietly in the teenager's lap but wore a worried expression. How many hours, Dewy wondered, had this baby spent in emergency rooms with their din and odors and people poking her? Carol had also brought Gerald with her so they could check his TB test. It was negative, but Gerald looked miserable and seemed spooked by the chaos all around him.

"How's the baby doing?" Dewy asked the big sister.

"She's getting worse," Cheryl said. "This morning she screamed for a long time. Mom wants to know if you got the results of the EEG yet. They did the test yesterday morning and Darryl had a screaming fit while they were doing it. Good girl!" she said to the baby.

"I'll go see if I can find the results right now." Dewy found nothing in the computer, so she called the EEG lab. The technician said that the neurologist hadn't yet looked at the study, but she was pretty sure there was no seizure activity during the baby's crying fit.

Carol was still on the phone when Dewy returned. The room was literally packed. Dr. Stone was counseling another family. Two kids waiting to be picked up by parents, one with a casted arm and one in a neck brace were horsing around. Merrill, Gerald, Cheryl and Baby Darryl all looked distressed.

The rain was still coming down in buckets and another car crash victim had just arrived in critical condition. The hospital administrator came to the ER to announce that he had notified the citywide emergency medical system that all ambulances would have to take their patients to other hospitals. There wasn't a bed left at CityStar. Dewy wondered if she'd survive her internship, let alone her ER rotation.

When Carol finally got off of the phone and Dr. Brody Jones finished giving her follow-up instructions for Merrill's mouth lacerations, Dewy approached her to tell her about Gerald's TB test.

Carol was more interested in the results of the baby's EEG, which Dewy didn't want to share until the official reading came through. She apologized that the EEG results and Gerald's lab work were still pending.

Carol glowered at Dewy. She also didn't seem very concerned about Merrill's teeth, perhaps because his father could make him pretty new ones. Dewy surmised that Carol was too frazzled at the moment to deal with any single one of her multiple kids' multiple problems. She demanded to be discharged immediately so she could go pick the other kids up from camp. She certainly wasn't going to let any of those "damn baby bus drivers in those damn baby buses with bad bald tires," transport her children on these soaked slick roads.

Dewy felt utterly useless as she watched the Farrells head for the exit with woozy Merrill swaying like a willow in the wind. She now knew that Merrill had spent his first three months of life in the neonatal intensive care unit, and Dewy wondered if he was the child who Carol was least attached to.

At the end of her shift, Dewy found the EEG results and one of Gerald's lab results in the computer. There was no seizure activity for the baby, and Gerald didn't show antibodies for the Epstein-Barr virus that caused mononucleosis. Carol didn't answer her phone, so Dewy sent her the new information through the patient portal.

Before she left, Dewy said hello to Liselle Grady at the triage desk. Liselle was just coming onto her shift, but she'd already heard that Merrill Farrell was one of the bus crash kids. Their conversation turned to the baby.

"Liselle," Dewy asked, "how did you know about the Farrell baby's visits to the other hospitals on the first night I saw her?"

"Let's just say that someone here has friends in the other hospitals," Liselle confessed.

Dewy explained why she thought Carol was hiding something that happened at Pine Meadow Medical Center.

"I'll see what I can find out. Now get out of here already," Liselle scolded. "You dayshift people look exhausted and you all need a shower." Liselle wrinkled her nose. "This whole place needs a shower. I never saw such mud and it smells like a swamp in here." Dewy wondered if she also stunk. She took a big sniff as she turned around to leave.

"Hey, Dewy, before you go, I just have to ask you where you get your scrubs? The whole staff is dying with jealousy and no one can find anything like them anywhere."

Dewy did a pirouette to show off her slinky copper top with leopard print pockets, and matching leopard print pants. Her glittery rust colored sneakers were the perfect accent. The copper color of her top almost matched the color of her golden-brown eyes.

"Thanks, Liselle. I got that shimmering silver set from a French website, and when my kid sister saw it, she was inspired. She's a fashion design student, and she made these scrubs and a few other sets for me. Aren't they the cat's meow?" Dewy did another pirouette. "Now my sister is entertaining becoming a medical fashion designer."

"Your sister should drop out of school and start making these scrubs right now. I'd be thrilled to be her marketing manager. Such a fabulous idea! Your scrubs make this dreary place a little brighter.

"Now please go home and get some sleep, and let's hope to not have any more bus crashes tonight on these foggy, flooded roads."

Chapter Fifteen

*D*ewy was back on the nightshift, working with Dr. Olga Volkov. There were several chest pain patients present, and Dr. Olga was helping her with the nuances of reading EKGs. Dewy had just finished giving a young couple the good news that the man's chest pain wasn't due to a heart attack, but a case of bad indigestion, when triage nurse Liselle beckoned her out of the room. She handed Dewy a chart.

"We had to get this one out of the waiting room pronto. This case might just be in your wheelhouse, Dr. Meadows. We don't know her name yet, so she's identified right now as Miss X. She's in room eight."

Upon entering the padded room, Dewy encountered an elderly tired-looking policeman and a young woman in party attire. Miss X was alternately sitting and standing. Her eyes were darting all over the room, and she kept swatting at whatever it was she was seeing, when she wasn't frantically fingering a glow stick necklace. She didn't acknowledge being spoken to. Dewy tried all of her languages, but the woman didn't seem to see or hear anything that was real.

"What do we know about her?" Dewy asked the policeman.

"A pub manager was checking on a long-locked lady's room and found her there, doing what you see her doing now. No purse, pockets or ID. We looked all over the place for a purse. None of the bar patrons claimed to know her or have noticed her when she came in.

There were no raves going on there or nearby, so who knows where she came from."

While it looked like a bad drug reaction, Dewy was also concerned that the delusions could be due to acute psychosis. She ordered bedside video monitoring, a drug screen, basic chemistries, and a sedative, should the woman show increased agitation.

Before she got her notes completed on Miss X, Dewy was assigned another police case. Liselle had labeled this one "Little Miss X." In room nine, Dewy found a young policewoman with a raggedy little girl slumped over in her lap. Matted hair concealed the child's face. She wore a dirty, tattered prairie dress, no shoes or socks. They'd soon find out she also had no underwear.

"She was found wandering around in the bus station, crying, about an hour ago," the policewoman said. "Not English speaking; hardly speaking at all. We offered her juice and cookies and she devoured them like she was starving. She fell asleep in the car on the way here and didn't awaken when I carried her in. It's like she's passed out. I checked our missing child database, but she doesn't fit the description of any locally missing kids."

As they laid the little girl down on the exam table, a black and white polka dot scarf around her neck became noticeable. Dewy slapped her hand to her chest and said "Unbelievable! A Hutterite! How in the world did she wind up here?"

"A what?" the policewoman asked.

"Officer, when she talked, did it sound kind of like German or Eastern European?"

"Something like that. I really couldn't tell, but I don't think it was Spanish or Asian."

"The Hutterites are an ethno-religious sect, kind of like the Amish of Pennsylvania, except they embrace modern technology.

They live in small isolated colonies in the Dakotas, Montana and western Canada. Most speak English, but some primarily speak Hutterish, a German dialect. I think they all learn Hutterish in their schools."

"I never heard of them. How do you know about them, Dr. Meadows?"

"My father was a geologist who helped mine operators find veins of gold. One summer, he took our family with him on an assignment in South Dakota, and there were Hutterite colonies around where we stayed. My father could communicate with them in German.

"We'd sometimes see them in stores. The women and girls all wore these long dresses and a black-and-white polka-dot headscarf, exactly like the one someone tied around this child's neck. The scarf distinguishes them from other fundamentalist sects that wear prairie dresses.

"You need to check the missing child reports where the Hutterites live. I bet everyone in the colony is out frantically searching for this girl. These people live for their colony first, their selves second."

"I'll get right on it," the policewoman said.

"Officer, could you first please stay for a few minutes as a witness to a sexual abuse evaluation? It would be best if I could get it done very gently, right now while she's zonked out like this, and then you can take the rape kit evidence with you. We have a special camera to document the trauma. We do have a rape team here, but by the time I could summon them, our little girl might not be sleeping so soundly and then she'd be traumatized again. I also need to draw blood and she'll likely wake her up when she gets poked. It breaks my heart to even try to imagine what she's been through. I'll alert social services to find her shelter."

When Dewy returned to room eight, the party dress patient was lying on the bed and staring at the ceiling. She was still fingering the glow stick necklace and she still occasionally swatted at things. Her toxicology screen came back positive for almost all of the party drugs that they could test for. Hopefully, she'd sleep it off and wake up in the real world.

Dr. Olga said sometimes the drugs precipitated acute psychotic breaks that didn't resolve when the drugs wore off. Dewy could only hope that this young woman would come back to Earth when her trip was over. Brody Jones might have to decide if she was sane.

The Hutterite child woke up just before the end of Dewy's shift. Her Tyrolean dialect was difficult to understand, but Dewy was able to glean that, "her name is Mila. She's six. A bad man took her and hurt her. They rode in a big blue truck every day. Her big sister is Emma. Her name for her colony is unintelligible to me." Dewy signed the case over to Brody as medically okay to go, but waiting for foster home placement, preferably German speaking.

Dewy was finishing up her notes when Liselle beckoned her into the privacy alcove. "I have some follow-up for you. Our Pine Meadow contact actually knew about the Farrell baby's case, not surprising since Carol is legendary wherever she goes.

"They did an endoscopic exam of Darryl's whole GI tract a few weeks ago, and they found a teeny-weeny hairball in her stomach. They figured that maybe one of the other kids was giving the baby things to eat, but it also seemed plausible that the baby mouthed a toy that was coincidentally contaminated with something one of the cats hacked up. Maybe the baby was sucking on a cat's tail. Who knows?

"Carol became almost civil when they showed her the hairball, but then, when there was no improvement in the baby's symptoms after the hairball was extracted, Carol's claws came out at a follow-up visit and she left in a rage.

"I wonder if that whole family isn't walking around with cat hair in their guts. I'll bet I eat a pound of dog hair annually with my two shedding mutts," Liselle mused.

Dewy smiled as she reminisced about smooching with her beagles. She hadn't lived at home for eight years, but she could still find beagle hair amidst her belongings.

Later, she was surprised to learn that there were actually calorie values assigned to human, cat and dog hair.

Chapter Sixteen

As soon as Dewy started the next nightshift, Molly Hudson showed up with three children. Merrill needed his sutures removed. His face was a colorful pallet of resolving bruises and he had a temporary bridge for front teeth. Little Laurel had a fever and a stuffy nose, and Carol was worried the baby would catch it. Gerald was getting worse. He was still running fever, his joints hurt, he was eating poorly, and he wasn't his usual, busy little self.

Molly reported that Carol had taken Gerald to an urgent care clinic over the weekend, and the physician there concurred that there was no known cure for cat scratch disease. It just had to run its course.

"Where's Carol now?" Dewy asked, expecting her to come charging in with the screaming infant at any moment.

"Carol's home with Darryl. She's trying a no-sound environment this week. She went to see an acoustic therapist, who tested to see if certain frequency sounds like white noise irritated or relaxed the baby. Darryl's heart rate was slowest with no sound. So now, there's no TV, no vacuuming, no conversation in the baby's presence, and the rest of the children can't quite be children. Carol didn't want to expose Darryl to the noise of the ER, but she wanted you to take another look at Gerald, so she sent me."

"How's the baby doing?" Dewy asked, as she pulled up Gerald's chart on the computer. Gerald's labs from his previous visit showed that he had antibodies to cat scratch bacteria, but they'd have to retest him in a few months to know if the antibodies represented old immunity or new infection. The test was of academic interest, but of no practical value to patients who had already recovered from the illness.

"The baby's the same, maybe worse, and Carol is getting desperate." Molly said. "She's recently consulted a naturopath, a Reiki master and an Ayurveda practitioner. I'm surprised she hasn't taken Darryl to her vet. As of yesterday, she's trying to treat the baby with aromatherapy. Now the house stinks of chamomile, lavender and cat, but Darryl is still having her screaming fits.

"Could Darryl's problem be due to an allergy?" Molly asked. "When I was a kid and I'd get spring allergies, I'd get this burning sensation on the roof of my mouth and deep in my ears. I'd walk around with my fingers in my ears and my tongue clucking against my palate all spring, until they did some testing and decided I had allergies. Then they gave me allergy pills, which finally relieved the burning.

"I suggested to Carol that maybe Darryl cries when she eats because her mouth burns, but Carol doesn't want to try allergy medicine because Darryl's already on reflux medicine. Carol may also not want to know if the baby could be allergic to cats. Still, I think the baby's crying started right when everything started to bloom in spring. She was a peaceful little baby for her first few months of life."

"That's a very good question, Mrs. Hudson. I suppose it's possible. I wonder though, why Carol is continuing the reflux medicine when it hasn't helped. I think it would be worthwhile to stop the reflux drugs and give Darryl a trial of Benadryl. That would be a pretty easy and safe thing to do. Why don't you tell Carol that I recommend she switch to Benadryl to see if the baby is having allergy symptoms?"

"I'll do that, Dr. Meadows. As much as Carol hates doctors, she seems to trust you. She wasn't going to have me bring the kids here unless you were the doctor on duty. She didn't like the doctor who sewed up Merrill's mouth. She said he looks like he's twelve and on top of that, he's arrogant. I'd give him credit for his sewing though. He did a good job on Merrill."

"Let's get those stitches out right now." Dewy had Merrill lie down on the exam table. "So, you're Merrill Ray. Do your sisters and brothers have middle names too?"

"I'm Laurel Kay," the younger Farrell child announced, "K as in kitty. And he's Gerald Jay," she said, pointing to her brother. "J as in jelly. And then, there's Cheryl May, Terrell Trey, Beryl Gay, and the baby is Darryl Fay."

"Well those are very pretty names," Dewy said, silently snickering as she worked to remove Merrill's stitches. "Do the kitties have middle names too?"

"Just us kids have middle names," Gerald said.

"I got a new kitty," Laurel said. "He's black and white and he has a mustache." She giggled. "His name is Beano."

"No it's not! It's Bilko," Gerald argued. "Terrell wanted to call him Bozo, but Mommy decided on Bilko. And he's a stupid cat, just like Bingo."

"No he's not," Merrill interjected between stitches. "He's just a kitten."

Dewy and Grandma Molly both rolled their eyes. "When did you get a new kitty?" Molly asked her grandchildren, as Dewy got the last stitch out of Merrill's lips.

Merrill felt his lips with his hand and tried to smile, something he hadn't been able to do for a week. It didn't go well, and his siblings laughed at his crooked grin. Dewy wondered if he had nerve damage.

With barely intelligible speech, Merrill said, "Mommy found the kitten on Friday. He was hanging out in the yard with Bingo. Mommy took him to the vet, and he didn't have a chip, so she said we could keep him. He's a sweet little kitty."

Merrill felt the inside of his lip with his tongue, and Dewy avoided handing him a mirror. He was still a scary looking mess.

"He's a pretty kitty," Laurel said. Then she sneezed and clear mucous dribbled onto her upper lip. Dewy checked her for cat scratches and swollen glands all over but found nothing of concern. Her throat wasn't red, and her lungs and ears were clear.

"Probably just a cold," she said to Molly as she lifted Laurel off the table and signaled to Gerald to climb on. You just need to try to get a lot of fluids into her, and let's recheck her if she develops other symptoms. And keep her away from the baby."

Gerald seemed lethargic. A sickly pallor had replaced his camp suntan. He complained of his knees and his hands hurting. The swollen lymph nodes in his neck and the one in his armpit seemed bigger, but he wasn't wincing and withdrawing like he did the last time. Was he getting used to the pain?

After Dewy finished his exam, Molly announced that she'd been reading about childhood malignancies. She was apparently avoiding the word cancer in front of the kids, but the look on Merrill's distorted face suggested he knew what she was talking about. He'd probably heard the word when he was the mystery bellyache patient. "Could it be lymphoma?" Molly asked. "I read that's the third most common childhood malignancy."

Dewy recalled Dr. Patel saying that the swollen glands of lymphoma weren't usually tender, so she shared that with Molly to try to reassure her, while she simultaneously wondered if Gerald might have lymphoma and cat scratch disease at the same time. He looked really ill. She asked Dr. Volkov for a consult.

"I don't like the way that child looks one bit," Dr. Olga said, after they exited the room. "He looks sicker to me than the typical cat scratch patient."

"Do you think we need to biopsy the big lymph node?" Dewy asked.

"Before we talk biopsy, repeat his labs, and get a blood culture. Test him for toxoplasmosis and get a chest x-ray, though his lungs sound clear. Sometimes lymphoma affects the lymph nodes in the chest which can be seen on x-ray."

Gerald's chest film looked okay, but his sed rate was higher and his blood cell counts were a little lower than the last time. Dr. Volkov was worried enough to recommend referral to a pediatric oncologist. The Farrells would have to go across town to where there were now pediatric specialists.

Dr. Volkov remarked, "it's really a shame that the hospital trustees opted to build the new children's hospital on the other side of town. I understand that's where the young families are moving to these days, but now we don't have pediatric specialists here on campus. On the other hand, Carol's distrust of our pediatric staff is probably the reason why she didn't go to the shiny new children's hospital but came to old CityStar instead."

Grandma Molly looked solemn when Dewy gave her the news. She imagined the scene of Molly telling Carol about an oncology consult and felt a knot in her stomach. She spent the rest of her shift just waiting for Carol to come storming into the ER and demanding that Gerald have his lymph node biopsied here and now. Dewy could hardly blame her if she did.

In the meantime, she took care of people with colds, cuts, coughs and wheezes, stomachaches, headaches, joint sprains, muscle strains, chest pains, fainting and strokes. She diagnosed leukemia in a homeless man who had been found unconscious on a park bench, and medication-induced kidney failure in a nursing home resident. She spent a few minutes here and there, reading about lymphoma in children and allergies in infants.

Doctors Dewy and Olga went to breakfast together when their shift was over. The conversation eventually got around to the Farrell baby. Dewy told Olga the story of the hairball. Dr. Olga admitted to smooching with her own dogs. "Dog love is the best love you can get in this life," she declared, and raised her coffee cup to toast dogs, *sobaki*, in Russian.

"To hairballs," Dewy toasted back, "but this case has me *smushchenny*." She resorted to Russian to express her confusion. I don't know if what's going on with that baby is internal or external. If they found one hairball in her, even though it was tiny, why couldn't she have another? Do small hairballs cause pain? If one of the cats is playing with her toys or leaving hairballs in her crib, or if one of the other kids is feeding her hairballs or boogers or who knows what, how do we know that she doesn't have some piece of something somewhere in her gut, or her airways, or somewhere in the soft tissues of her mouth or throat?"

"Were you able to examine under her tongue?" Dr. Olga asked. "Most of us don't bother to look at the floor of the mouth when we're looking at throats, but we should."

"I didn't," Dewy admitted. "You're right. I wonder if they did that when they scoped her upper GI tract. What if she has some teensy foreign body lodged in her tongue or gums that hurts when she swallows?"

"Well that would make more sense than something in her airways. If there were something in the airway, she'd have a cough or wheezing. Something in the larynx would make her voice hoarse."

"Her voice is hoarse, but I assumed that's because she screams a lot."

"Well, then maybe we do need to look at her airways. I can't imagine Carol will be gung-ho for bronchoscopy under anesthesia. Maybe we need to start with manually examining her mouth. If that's good, let's try imaging of her head and neck. See if you can use your charm to get Carol to agree to that. You probably want MRI because a single CT scan in a young infant significantly increases the risk of subsequently developing a lethal tumor. Of course, she'd have to be sedated for MRI, so Carol won't like that.

"I don't know if that baby will ever get help if someone doesn't take a personal interest in her case and pursue an answer, assuming there is an answer. However, you're here to learn about the spectrum of human maladies, Dewy, not to be someone's personal physician. There are plenty of doctors in this city who could be Carol's personal physician, if she didn't bite their heads off. You're taking on a difficult task, and I admire you for that. Just don't let the challenge consume you. Personally, I'd rather take care of a dozen drunken dregs then spend one minute with that crazy cat lady.

"Also, keep in mind that the Farrell's health insurer undoubtedly has someone monitoring their account, ready to pounce on any reimbursement they can deny. I'll bet Carol's on the phone arguing for her benefits on an ongoing basis, so we need to be sure that we're not doing unnecessary testing or over-treating what may only be a bad case of colic, or the hospital won't get paid.

"CityStar spends a fortune fighting for reimbursement from insurers who have a million reasons as to why they won't pay for the care we give. As a matter of fact, the hospital has more people writing appeals of reimbursement denials than they have doctors in the ER trying to save lives. And, if Carol's insurer doesn't pay the bills, then Carol will get the bills, and the hospital will have to fight with Carol to get reimbursed. I doubt there's a person in the billing department who would want that job."

"Wow! That's an issue I better start learning to consider," Dewy said. "When you practiced in the old Soviet Union, you probably didn't have to worry about insurance companies."

"No, I didn't worry about insurance companies back then. What I worried about then was if we had the tools to treat the patients. We were always out of basic supplies and drugs, the x-ray units were always breaking, and compared to healthcare in the rest of the world, the medical system in the U.S.S.R. was extremely backward. I didn't even know how backward it was until I got to the States and saw that the Soviets were decades behind."

"How did you get from the U.S.S.R. to the U.S., Dr. Olga? My Russian grandfather said the old Soviets didn't like to let their more educated people out."

"No, they didn't, but they did like to get rid of people who might have genetic problems. I had a son who had severe medical problems. We never did know why. When he was six, he had the mental age of a two-year-old, and he had vision and kidney problems. Genetic testing was just taking off in the 1980s. Even when we got to the States, the testing wasn't sophisticated enough to identify a genetic defect in my son. They didn't even do genetic testing in the U.S.S.R. back then, but the Soviet authorities, under the guise of compassion, allowed us to emigrate because they wanted to purge their population of genetically defective people. My son died from his multiple problems at age eleven, but I will always be grateful to him for being our passport out of the Soviet Union. Had he not been profoundly disabled, they would never have let us go.

"After I got to the States, I did some catch-up training in a hospital in New York City where I saw a few other Russian families with some very weird medical issues. They were all recent immigrants. Those were the only people the Soviets were letting out back then."

"How sad! *Tak zhal,*" Dewy offered her sympathy in Russian. "I am so sorry for the tragic loss of your son."

"Thank you, Dewy. Anyway, you need to be sure you carefully document your rationale for any testing or treatment we administer to the Farrells, or the hospital will surely be at war with their insurance company, or maybe worse, with that crazy cat lady."

Chapter Seventeen

*O*n her next dayshift, Dewy was surprised to find herself working side by side with Dr. Brody Jones and an attending she hadn't worked with before. Brody had traded a nightshift for a dayshift with the third-year resident who needed the day off because his widowed father was undergoing surgery. The attending physician, Dr. Debra Yeager, hadn't yet worked with either Dewy or Brody, and she wasn't happy about having two interns staffing the ER on her first day back from vacation.

Triage nurse Xray assured the attending physician that the interns were both very competent and could function pretty independently. "Brody Jones is super speedy, and he loves to sew." X said. "Dewy Meadows is super slow, but she's multilingual and especially good with difficult patients. She's actually been taking care of Carol Farrell's kids."

Dr. Yeager stopped in her tracks, looking like she'd been smacked. She tossed her long gray braid over her shoulder. "Please don't tell me the Farrells are back in our ER. Did they get booted out of all the other hospitals in this city? Which kid is she here for; not Merrill I pray?"

Xray said, "would you believe we've seen four of the kids in the past few weeks? A little girl with a cold, a boy with cat scratch disease, surprise, surprise, poor Merrill with facial trauma, and a new baby that screams a lot that no one can figure out.

"Carol first came here for the baby and Liselle gave the case to Dr. Meadows, and she somehow connected with Carol. Now, Carol calls ahead to find out if she's here before she brings the kids in, except in Merrill's case. Maybe you heard about the camp bus crash. Poor Merrill was one of the kids on that bus, so that's how he wound up back at CityStar. He was one of the lucky ones; he only smashed his face and lost a few teeth."

"It's hard to think of Merrill as a lucky kid between his asthma, the weird parasite thing and the mother from hell. If Dr. Meadows can get along with that woman, she can have my job right now." Dr. Yeager said. "It was so peaceful around here for the past two years that the Farrells weren't in this ER every week. What's with the baby anyway?"

"Nobody knows," Xray answered. "We think Carol has been to a host of doctors and every hospital in town. The baby's had a barrage of tests, and colic is the working diagnosis. Our young Dr. Meadows actually seems obsessed with the case, so I'm sure she'll try to pick your brains, and who better than Dr. Yeager, always the attack dog when it comes to medical mysteries. Put on your sunglasses, here she comes." Xray turned back to his triage desk.

In brilliant fuchsia scrubs with satiny navy accents and glittery navy sneakers, a svelte waif of a woman introduced herself to Dr. Debra Yeager as Dr. Dewy Meadows. "I've got a puzzling rash in room five. It's an eight-year-old girl with a cough and multiple red streaks on her back; it kind of looks like abuse. Would you mind taking a look?"

Dr. Yeager and the mother of the child conversed in Vietnamese for a moment, and Dr. Yeager turned to Dewy and said, "coining. To break up chest congestion, they rub the skin overlying the lungs with the edge of a coin. It increases blood flow to the region.

Americans do it with Vicks vapor rub. Acupuncturists do it with cupping. Coining is a relatively harmless home remedy in Southeast Asia, and it maybe helps to some small degree."

Dr. Yeager examined the child and then talked to the mother in Vietnamese some more. She advised Dewy to discharge the patient with an inhaler for nighttime coughing.

"I wonder why Xray didn't assign this case to you, since you obviously speak her language," Dewy said after they left the room.

"Because the mother does speak English. I just like to practice my Vietnamese. My mother was an army nurse in Vietnam in the 1960s, and she made friends there and became fluent in the language. When I was growing up, we visited her friends during summers and I also learned the language. Vietnam is a gorgeous country and I like to vacation there.

"I'm glad you called me in on that case. I've seen parents get charged with abuse because coining does make it appear that the skin has been traumatized, when all the parents are trying to do is help their kids feel better. On the other hand, if you see marks on a child that you think could be suspicious, don't assume innocence or guilt until you've thoroughly investigated."

Dewy wondered if Dr. Yeager had already heard about the Darryl Farrell case. The Farrells had become a prime topic of staff gossip during the past few weeks, and Dewy was eager to have the opportunity to garner another opinion from a seasoned physician, if they could just find some time to chat. As it turned out, there would be no downtime for the staff of CityStar ER that balmy summer Sunday.

The elderly patient leading the incoming parade arrived by ambulance. He had reportedly thrown up and passed out on the sixth hole of a golf course. The next two arrived by private vehicle with severe stomach cramps. They had been playing the same course.

One of the patients reported that a large legal firm had rented the facilities of a private country club to hold their annual charity golf tournament. Before the first tee-off, participants were treated to a catered breakfast featuring pancakes, omelets, bacon, ham, fruit and lots of trimmings. After seeing a dozen victims, Dr. Yeager deduced that the sickest people had eaten the most ham, and the healthy people who transported the sick ones hadn't eaten any ham.

CityStar Hospital was the closest ER to the country club. Over the next two shifts, the ER staff would see twenty-seven lawyers and paralegals with staphylococcal food poisoning, most of them needing intravenous hydration. Dewy and Brody spent their shift deciding who needed another liter of IV hydration, and who was in good enough shape to take their erupting intestines home.

As they would learn from Debra Yeager, the nature of the illness indicated it wasn't the staph bacteria that had made these people sick, but a toxin produced by the bacteria. Antibiotics had no impact on the toxin, and sufferers could expect to recover in a day or two, after the toxin was cleared from their guts, as long as they didn't get too dehydrated.

Ultimately, the health department determined that a cutting board was contaminated with the toxin when it was used to prepare an uncooked ham, and then it was inadequately cleaned before the baked ham was put back on it for slicing. The unfortunate caterer would probably wind up dealing with multiple lawsuits because one of her employees had made an unforgiveable mistake.

Dr. Debra Yeager was in conference with health department officials when it was time for the interns to sign their patients over to the nightshift. As they exited the ER, Brody said "I was going to ask you to dinner, Dewy, but we both stink. Would you meet me after we've had time to shower and change?"

Dewy figured there might not be another opportunity to socialize with Brody when he went back to his normal schedule, and she was a little curious about him, so she said yes. She went back to her apartment to clean up and they met in the pizzeria next to the hospital campus a half-hour later.

Chapter Eighteen

"You didn't really think I was going to take you to dinner in a pizza joint, did you?" Brody bragged, as he ushered her out the door where a cab was waiting to take them to an upscale restaurant she had only heard about."

Dewy hadn't thought this was going to be a date. She thought they were just two weary interns grabbing a meal together between work and sleep. She wondered if she should tell Brody up front that she was already in a committed relationship, except that she wasn't sure if she still was.

Dewy and Alex had lived together their last year of medical school, but they had chosen different career paths that had taken them far apart. Alex was determined to be a cancer researcher and had opted for training in a program that didn't provide Dewy with the clinical experience she sought. So, they had amicably agreed to separate and see where their respective career paths took them, although Alex seemed more eager to separate than did Dewy.

Several weeks later, Alex didn't seem to be missing Dewy at all, while Dewy was wondering if there was a psychiatry program that would allow her to transfer so that they could be together for her second year of residency. Since starting her ER rotation, she had just been too busy and too tired to even try to sort out her feelings about her relationship with Alex. She was hoping that time and the separation would help her to clarify things.

Until she and Brody started talking shop, the cozy booth, the expensive menu, and the impeccable service all made Dewy uncomfortable. For one thing, she could live on peanut butter and jelly sandwiches for all she cared about food. For another, she didn't perceive Brody as a potential friend, and didn't know why she had said yes to his invite. She had only meant to be social. She did like champagne though, and she was both surprised and delighted when Brody ordered a very expensive bottle.

"How'd you know I like champagne?" Dewy asked.

"Lucky guess. Your style says you have champagne taste." Brody winked. "I heard you and Nurse Hana talking about needing a glass of bubbly at the end of a shift."

Dewy wondered what else Brody had ease-dropped on. "So, whatever happened to that case last week of the woman who OD'd on a smorgasbord of club drugs?"

"That was bizarre. When she finally woke up from her bad trip, she was beyond humiliated to find herself in an ER, and she was hysterical over having lost her purse. Turns out, she's a psychiatric social worker who takes care of patients with addiction disorders. She claimed she went to a rave just to see what her patients were experiencing, and she didn't even know how she got so wasted, or for how many days she was in never-never-land; or so she claimed. The psych resident discharged her without a follow-up; his risk."

"What ever happened to the little Hutterite girl? Did they find a German-speaking family to foster her? I meant to look up her discharge summary, but I just never got to it."

"They found her real family in Montana, thanks to you. That was so fortunate that you were there that shift and that the police followed up on your lead. How'd you know about the Hutterites? Nobody else in the ER on my shift had ever heard of them."

Dewy told Brody the story of her summer in South Dakota, and then the story she had been repeating her entire life about how she came to be multilingual. She also told him she was super focused on her training and gathering data for her linguistics research, and she didn't think she had time to date at this point in her career.

Brody said he felt the same way about not currently having the time or the energy to be in a relationship, but it would be nice to have someone to go to dinner with now and then.

He then told Dewy his story. He'd grown up in L.A. His father was a plastic surgeon who became known far and wide for doing exceptionally nice work on noses. He became known as Nosy Jones, the doctor darling of cover girls and starlets, some of whom got more than a new nose out of the arrangement.

Brody's mother divorced him when Brody was nine and his sister was seven, and his dad married an actress who divorced him sixteen months later to marry her costar. Brody didn't really like his father's second, third, or fourth wife, or his circle of rich and famous friends. He didn't find those Hollywood people any more interesting than all of the ordinary people he was now working with on a daily basis. "The Hollywood people seem crazier than normal people."

"So, you're not planning on following in your father's footsteps?" Dewy remarked, as she tried to decide whether Brody's perfect nose and his cleft chin were natural. Those features seemed more manly than did his rosy round face with its upturned mouth.

"If and when I become a father, I plan to take very good care of my children, unlike the father who abandoned me," Brody lamented. "Although I do love looking at people's facial features and thinking about how I could make them look better, hopefully, that's the only thing I have in common with my father. He's a real opportunist. I just want to make everyone beautiful. That sounds corny, doesn't it?"

MATTHEW MCLACHLAN LIVES IN ASTORIA, Queens. He is the resident playwright for Ruddy Productions in New York City.

Contact Information

● ● ●

Website: MatthewMclachlan.com
E-mail address: MMclachlan123@gmail.com

Made in the USA
Middletown, DE
20 August 2022

70998036R00116

Dewy didn't know how to respond, so she changed the subject. "Speaking of parents and kids, let me see what you think of my latest theory about the Farrell crybaby." She told Brody the hairball story and her concern about a foreign body hiding somewhere in the baby's oral tissues.

"That's an interesting theory," Brody responded. "I never gave it much thought before, but growing up, I had a gray Siamese cat named Shadow, and I kissed that cat all the time. We got her when she was a kitten when I was nine, and she was my best friend, especially after my dad took off. She was a really sweet cat, smart and affectionate.

"I wonder if I have hairballs. I now have a cat named Hairy Potter. He's a Maine coon, quite the enormous fellow. His tail is as big as my mom's whole cat, and my mom's cat is a big fat calico. Hairy Potter sheds like a maniac and his hair is in everything I own, in addition to maybe being in my gut."

"I thought pets weren't allowed in hospital housing," Dewy said.

"Cruelly true, but I live in a cat friendly high-rise right next to the campus. As long as Daddy still pays the bills, nothing can come between Hairy Potter and me.

"I think there's a chapter in one of my surgery textbooks about foreign bodies in unfortunate places. Let me take a look at that, and I'll let you know if I find anything relevant."

Dewy didn't insist on paying her own share when the bill came. It was way beyond her means. She wondered if she had misread Brody's smugness. He seemed to have a soft side. Perhaps it was just his beard deficiency that provoked his macho swagger.

Chapter Nineteen

ewy was on dayshift when Xray warned her that Carol Farrell had signed into the ER and wanted Dewy to see Merrill, Gerald, and Baby Darryl. Merrill's face wasn't healing well. Carol didn't like Dr. Armstrong, the pediatric oncologist that had provided a consult for Gerald, and Baby Darryl was still screaming. Her screaming fits were happening more often, every day, and she was no longer gaining weight like she had been. There was no screaming at the moment. Xray commented about Merrill's face looking quite awful.

Dewy found the oncologist's notes in the computer. Gerald had been seen the previous day and the oncologist repeated his labs. The numbers came back essentially the same as his last ER visit. Lymphoma was considered unlikely, and the cat scratch diagnosis fit all of his symptoms. If he wasn't turning the corner in another week, or if he got worse, Dr. Armstrong wanted the Farrells to come back for a recheck. It was also noted that Carol wasn't happy with the plan. She wanted a more immediate answer.

Dewy could really sympathize with Carol, but she also understood the doctor's conservative approach. Still, worrying that your child could have cancer while the doctors are taking a wait-and-see attitude, had to be very disconcerting, especially for a parent as stressed and anxious as Carol.

Dewy felt anxious about Gerald too. It was a long time for this little boy to be so sick. She tried to call the oncologist to find out what the specialist really thought but couldn't get through. Dr. Armstrong was in a sterile room doing a bone marrow biopsy on another little kid with suspected cancer. Dewy shuddered to think what a pediatric oncologist's days must be like. She had no idea what to say to Carol about this wait-and-see approach, when she herself wanted an answer right now.

Before she got to the Farrells, she was able to catch Dr. Yeager for a quick consult about Merrill's drooping face. The attending said they needed to review his x-rays because facial nerve injuries were associated with temporal bone fractures. "It's not unusual for progressive nerve damage to show up after the injury," Dr. Debra counseled. "Injured nerves can recover if they haven't been completely severed, but it can take months or even years. Recovery is quicker in kids, but you have to advise them to be patient."

"What happens if the nerve doesn't recover?" Dewy asked.

"Good question. I think there are some delicate surgical remedies like nerve transplantation. I don't even know who does that kind of thing around here, a neurosurgeon, or maybe an orofacial surgeon; but If Carol isn't inclined to wait, you might want to set up a consult with Dr. Chang, the pediatric neurosurgeon over at the children's hospital. He's relatively new to CityStar, so probably not on Carol's enemy list. Let him decide if it's in his domain. You need to get this child's hearing tested too, if there is a temporal bone fracture.

"Now that I think about it, set up a consult anyway, because while we wait to see if the nerve recovers on its own, the muscles of the face could atrophy and leave this little guy with a scary looking face. He might need some physical therapy and the injury needs to be monitored. Your ER rotation ends soon, Dewy, and our ER isn't the place for this problem to be managed, even if you were still going to be here."

Just as Dewy was about to run the screaming baby's case by Dr. Yeager, the attending physician got paged away to resuscitate an electrocution case. Xray had learned from the ambulance attendants that the teenager was retrieving a basketball that landed in a construction site when he tripped over a live wire that should never have been there. The senior resident was also attending the code, so Dewy seemed to be on her own to deal with Carol and three little kids she had no good answers for.

Nurse Gus stopped her before she entered the room. "I didn't get a blood pressure on any of them because I can't find the pediatric cuffs. On the assumption that someone walked out of here with the whole box of them, X is trying to find out where we can get more. Sorry!"

Gus continued, "Gerald says his knees hurt. His temp is one-o-one, though they're giving him Tylenol around the clock. Merrill's face does not look good, poor kid. The baby's quiet right now, no fever. Carol sounds like she might have a cold, but she denied that anyone else at home is currently sick. The little girl Laurel is recovered from her cold."

Dewy wondered if Gerald could have a cold on top of his cat scratch disease. Maybe that's why he still had fever. She looked up the notes on Merrill's bus trauma. Brody Jones had ordered skull and facial films at the time of the accident, and they were read as normal. She ran to the imaging department and asked the attending radiologist to review the films. He confirmed that there were no fractures, just soft tissue swelling on the lower half of the face.

Upon entering the treatment room, Dewy smelled menthol, which Carol was rubbing on Gerald's painful joints. Carol looked haggard, almost older than when Dewy had last seen her. Her obnoxious voice did sound nasal and Dewy wondered if she had been crying. Gerald still looked sickly, and Merrill's twisted smile was definitely a cause for concern. The discoloration and swelling of his face were almost gone, and his dental bridge looked natural, but if he tried to smile, the right corner of his mouth turned down and it looked like he was snarling. There was drool on his chin. The baby wasn't crying but she looked unhappy. There was an intense wariness to her facial expression as she scrutinized her surroundings. She must have come to associate the ER with torture.

Dewy methodically examined each of the children. She explained to Carol that she wanted to feel the baby's gums and tongue to be sure there wasn't some little piece of something stuck in there. She put on a glove and felt all around the baby's mouth, which Darryl tolerated better than she should have. She seemed too tired to fight like a healthy baby would normally do. "Has she been this sedate today?" Dewy asked.

"I think the screaming episodes exhaust her," Carol said, "and she's had two big ones already today, one at six a.m. and one with her last bottle. I also wondered if there could be something stuck in her gums, so we took her to one of the dental offices that Harold makes teeth for, and they took x-rays. Everything looked normal and her baby teeth are ready to pop.

"I've now tried every colic remedy known to humanity except acupuncture," Carol exclaimed, "and I have an appointment with a pediatric acupuncturist next week. I also took Darryl to an ear, nose and throat specialist at University Hospital earlier this week because her voice is getting more and more hoarse. She's now scheduled to have her airways scoped under sedation tomorrow, to see if there's something in her airways that hurts when she swallows. If you have any other ideas, Dr. Meadows, I'd love to hear about them. I don't like repeatedly sedating this baby, but she just keeps getting worse and no one can help us. Even the Internet is out of colic remedies."

"I wish I had another idea for you, Mrs. Farrell. I was just going to suggest checking Darryl's airways because her oral exam gave no clues. I'm glad to know her mouth was checked with x-rays and probably better with dental x-rays than we can do here. Thanks for letting me know about these other avenues of investigation you've undertaken. I'd truly like to be the physician who helps Darryl and solves this mystery, so any information you can share with me could give me a helpful clue."

Remarkably, Carol, the bona fide blabbermouth, said nothing. She was obviously looking for help in lots of places, but it seemed as though she was challenging each diagnostician to come to their own conclusion. Only after Dewy would suggest a diagnostic approach, would Carol reveal that it had already been done. What else besides the hairball was she hiding, or was this just this her way of controlling things? Was it all part of her domineering personality disorder, or was this her way of testing a physician? If so, she was good at it.

Was testing or controlling the physician what really smart psychiatric patients liked to do? Was psychiatry a battle of wits, a form of mind war? Dewy finally broke away from her thoughts and doubts. "So, are you still giving Darryl the reflux medicine?"

"I stopped those medicines and I took your suggestion about a trial of Benadryl. I gave it to her for five days. Maybe she slept more, but it did nothing to stop her screaming fits, so I stopped it as well."

Dewy didn't know what else to say about the baby. "So, what's been happening with Gerald?" she asked.

"We did not like Dr. Armstrong. She was too matter of fact and she said his illness looks like cat scratch disease to her. She'd only consider biopsy if his blood counts deteriorate. She wants to recheck him in another week so she can make more money. What does she care if this little boy lies in his bed crying for another week and loses more weight? I'm taking him to another oncologist on Friday."

Dewy was wishing Grandma Molly hadn't kicked the hornet's nest of lymphoma, but it was the fear of missing a cancer diagnosis that prompted the consult. Carol was probably right to get a second opinion. "Was there something you hoped I can do for Gerald while you're waiting to see the specialist?"

"Gerald needs something for pain. He's up crying in the middle of the night. I've been alternating Tylenol with Advil. I've tried ice and a heating pad, warm baths, and rubbing his knees with tiger balm. I've tried massage and favorite movies and anything else I can do to distract him, but he's still up crying in the middle of the night. Between him and the baby, I haven't had a decent night's sleep for weeks. I am so sick and tired of medical problems that you damn doctors can't solve. At least you ought to be able to help his pain."

Dewy had done enough studying to understand that cat scratch disease could cause nasty joint pain, especially in the knees, and it could last for up to six weeks. She didn't tell Carol that sometimes the joint pain becomes chronic, but that was more likely in adults.

She reviewed the doses that Carol was using for the over-the-counter pain relievers, and they were entirely appropriate. She really didn't want to give this child a narcotic, but it seemed like the humane thing to do under the circumstances. Gerald looked miserable and if he wasn't rubbing his knees, he was rubbing his wrists.

With trepidation, she gave Carol a prescription for a small bottle of liquid morphine, so Gerald could get a few night's sleep before his next doctor's appointment. Dewy would be greatly relieved if Gerald's medical dilemma were taken out of her hands. She turned her attention to Merrill.

As hard as he tried, Merrill couldn't smile on the right, nor could he squeeze his right eye shut. He also had trouble pronouncing the letters b, f, m, p, and w, with lips that weren't closing well. Carol said he was having difficulty eating and drinking. Dewy explained the need for follow-up with a neurosurgeon while Carol's demeanor went from despair to anger.

"Well you're no help at all. I don't even know why I came here today," Carol griped. "And it will cost my insurance company thousands. This sucks and you're all a bunch of asshole quacks," she barked as she gathered up her children and stormed out of the ER.

Dewy regretted trying to take on this family's issues. She should have just referred them to their family doctor, or a doctor they didn't already despise. She was in way over her head. At that moment, she hated that she was driven to psychoanalyze everyone. It was a compulsion she couldn't control. Some circuit in her brain kept firing and she couldn't find the switch to turn it off.

Her sister Daisy had a compulsion to hear song lyrics pop into her head in response to whatever was said to her, but Daisy knew how to turn her compulsion off.

Her half-sister Dahlia also had a compulsion. She imagined everyone she met in different clothing. Dahlia also claimed she couldn't overcome this obsession; she just had to mentally redress people.

Dewy's stepfather had a compulsion to look at rocks, whether they were on the roadside, in a mine, or in a glass dish on someone's coffee table. How many times had her family arrived late to some function because Daddy Dave had to pull off the road to check out a rock formation?

Her mother had a compulsion to say her daughters' names in at least three languages. Carolena's favorite for her was in English, Farsi and Mandarin, *Dewy, Jaleh, Lushui de.*

Dewy grew up thinking her whole family was nuts until learning that compulsions were normal and not always negative. Negative compulsions prompted people to repetitively engage in useless behavior that interfered with healthy living. Nail biting, pimple popping, or repetitively checking to see if one flushed the toilet, were negative compulsions; but without positive compulsive behaviors, humans wouldn't be driven to accomplish great things.

Dewy's compulsive persona took over. She'd try to somehow follow-up on the Farrell case, not give up. She was compelled to see it to a conclusion. At the same time, she wondered if she was really cut out to be a doctor, and why she had chosen a career where she would always be dealing with people who were miserable.

The good news that shift was that the electrocuted kid survived, though no one could say for sure if he'd ever be the same. Dewy wondered if that was good news, or not.

Chapter Twenty

Xray flashed a mischievous grin when he approached Dr. Brody Jones on a busy Friday afternoon. "I've got a little girl with a hand laceration for you. Someone dropped scissors into the crayon bin at camp and she got cut trying to find purple. She's here with her grandmother who says her vaccines are all up to date."

Brody took the tablet, looked at the chart long enough to see that it was Beryl Farrell, and handed it right back to Xray. "I really don't want to get any more involved with this family. Right now, I'm thinking they're going to sue me for Merrill's lip lacerations, as if somehow it was me that injured the nerve instead of the bus crash."

Xray pushed the chart right back at Brody and steered him into the privacy alcove. "Sorry, Dude. The docs here today have a worse history with the Farrells than you do, the physician assistant is tied up in the trauma room, the second-year resident is helping the medical student, and you're up for the next laceration. And this little Farrell kid is here with Grandma Molly, so you won't have to contend with 'she-who-must-not-be-named.'

"Maybe, if you become a successful plastic surgeon, you'll be able to turn away the difficult patients; but here, whether we like these people or not, we do our best to take care of them. We try to see every human being who comes here for help as if they could be a member of our own family, even the downtrodden, the angry and the crazy ones."

Brody couldn't decide what was making his cheeks burn, being lectured by this smartass nurse, or fearing the wrath of the crazy cat woman if his suturing results came out lousy. He had to conjure up his most pleasant self to greet the Farrells. He wanted to bolt when he walked into the room and found Grandma Molly with the hairball crybaby sitting in her lap, though Darryl wasn't crying at the moment. Had Xray deliberately not warned him about the baby? Relief washed over him when Molly indicated that Beryl was his only patient.

"The camp nurse thought it was too deep for steri-strips. Carol's taking her son Gerald to an oncologist right now, so I was babysitting for Darryl when the camp director called. I didn't see the cut, because it was bandaged when I got to the camp. Is it bad?"

"It doesn't hurt anymore," Beryl said, as Brody checked her hand. The cut was clean, but it ran across her palm and needed a minimum of four sutures. Beryl was able to flex and extend all of her fingers. She could tell the difference between sharp and dull with her eyes closed, so Brody was confident there were no damaged tendons or nerves.

"Not deep, but without stitches it will keep opening up because of where it is and how we use our hands. There will be tension on the stitches, so we're going to have to splint that hand for about ten days." He took a photo of the cut to put in her chart.

Beryl seemed cooperative until Brody went to numb up the skin. Then she got squirmy.

In his short time as an ER doctor, Brody had already repaired dozens of lacerations, and he'd simply ordered sedation for uncooperative kids. "Better to knock them out than to have them scared of needles and doctors for the rest of their lives," an instructor had said when he was a medical student in the ER. "You can do better work when the patient isn't wriggling."

Another mentor had said, "Order sedation if you want to make a ton of money for the hospital, and risk some kid having a respiratory arrest due to these sedative drugs; but if the kid is older than six, it's high time they learn to tolerate a few needle pricks."

Brody didn't know which of the two ER physicians to believe until he had an encounter with a six-year-old with a chin laceration who tried to bite him. He had also since learned that about ten percent of the population was genetically needle phobic. Such people have strong bodily reactions to the sight of blood or needles, and it wasn't necessarily something they could control.

Brody hadn't previously given much thought to how much more time, staffing, and cost was involved in sedating a child, and the thought of keeping the Farrells around long enough for the baby to start screaming gave him pause. He tried to be social with Grandma Molly while waiting for the numbing cream he applied to Beryl's hand to take effect. After some small talk about the hot summer, he reluctantly asked about the other kids.

"This baby here still screams a couple of times a day. Yesterday, the ENT doctor at University Hospital scoped her airways and everything was normal. Now her voice is even more hoarse.

"Gerald's doing poorly with his cat scratch disease; that's why Carol took him to an oncologist today for another opinion. He's still running fever and I've never before seen that child so inactive. Carol just called to tell me they're going to biopsy one of the lymph nodes now, and hopefully we'll get an answer soon.

"Merrill sees a neurosurgeon for his facial droop in three weeks. That's the soonest they could get him in. The other kids at camp have been kind to him because they've all been rattled by the bus crash.

Seeing their campmates and counselors in casts, on crutches, and in neck braces has been sobering for these kids, but Carol's really worried that Merrill will be teased when he goes back to school. He's pretty sensitive, so he's very upset about his droopy face and his speech and drooling. He doesn't want to talk, smile or eat. Carol's trying to get another consult with an oral surgeon who's a client of her husband's dental lab.

"You're the doctor who repaired Merrill's lip lacerations, aren't you?"

Brody wondered if his flushed face was obvious. The pictures that Nurse Gus had taken of Merrill and uploaded into his chart, showed a very asymmetric face. Looking at the photo made Brody feel nervous and defensive.

"I saw a picture of Merrill, poor kid. I'm afraid the trauma that injured his lips and teeth maybe also smashed some small nerves around his mouth. Nerves can recover, so hopefully he'll get his nice smile back." Brody realized he finished that statement with a smile, which made him feel awkward, so he quickly turned back to Beryl to see if she was less sensitive. He gently poked the skin with the small needle he hoped to inject the numbing agent with.

"Owie, owie!" She pulled her hand back.

"This topical stuff never works well enough on kid's hands, too many nerve endings," Brody declared. "I don't want to traumatize her, so I think we need to sedate her to repair the laceration properly," he told Molly, "with your permission of course."

"Whatever you have to do, Doctor. It is her dominant hand, so we need a good repair," Molly agreed, but her tone wasn't as convincing as her words. Brody wondered if Molly was as afraid of Carol as he was. How ridiculous, he thought, for so many professionals and the woman's own mother to be so terrorized by this crazy cat lady.

Brody wrote orders for a pediatric sedation protocol and went to check on other patients while he waited for Beryl to go to la-la land. Shortly thereafter, Gus beckoned him out of room four to tell him that Beryl was raising a ruckus in the suture room. Neither Brody nor Gus had previously seen the paradoxical agitation that the sedative occasionally causes.

Dr. Yeager got called into the room. She informed Brody, Gus, and Molly that while the vast majority of patients are readily sedated by the quick-acting drug midazolam, a few become agitated and aggressive. An antidote was given to Beryl, and within a few minutes she calmed down. She was unaware that moments ago, she had been flailing, kicking, and acting like a cornered wild animal. She was still too scared to hold still.

"Now what do I do?" Brody asked the attending physician.

"If she won't cooperate for local anesthesia," Dr. Yeager said, "we can sedate her with old-fashioned chloral hydrate. It takes longer for it to start working and to wear off, so we'll have to keep her here longer to monitor her until she's fully awake.

"I know it's seems crazy to make such a big production for maybe just a few sutures, but I think it's for the best. In my early ER days, no one sedated a child for such a simple procedure. We'd just hold them down, even if it meant tying them up or having multiple adults sit on them. Later on, we even used a little straight jacket to restrain them with.

"A few years ago, I had an uninsured family insist that we repair a toddler's cheek laceration without sedation because of the cost. Of course, you can't really keep a cheek from moving if the child is screaming. We had to blindfold the little boy so he couldn't see hands coming towards him, and hold his mouth closed with gauze between his teeth to keep the cheek still enough to close the wound.

I'll bet that poor kid still has nightmares. I'm so glad we don't do that anymore, though some ERs still do."

Molly gave the go ahead for them to try again to sedate her granddaughter. Beryl conked out appropriately and Brody repaired the wound without further difficulty. He returned to check on her status, just as the baby started to cry.

"That's her hunger cry," Molly said as she took out a bottle from the diaper bag. She was about to mix the formula powder up with tap water when Gus handed her bottled water.

"We don't drink the tap water here," he said. "They put extra disinfectant in our tanks."

"That reminds me," Molly said. "Carol mixes Darryl's formula up at home with tap water, and I was reading that lead in the water can cause abdominal pain. I told Carol she should get their water tested, but she said they get it checked every year and it's fine, and if there was a water problem, all of the kids would be sick. I don't know though. The other kids drink juice and soda, but almost never a glass of water. Carol even puts juice in their water bottles for camp. Do you think Darryl could have lead poisoning?"

"That's a good question," Brody responded, but he had no idea what the answer was. "Do the Farrells have municipal water, or do they have their own well?"

"Well water. That's why they get it checked every year."

"Let me see if our attending doctor knows what kind of water issues have been seen in this city. She's lived here much longer than I have."

With Beryl still zonked, Brody hoped there'd be enough time to get an answer to Molly's question. Until he finally caught up with Dr. Yeager, he tried looking up well water contaminants between seeing other patients. There were many things that could get into people's wells, and he realized it would take hours of study, if not months, to learn about all of the effects of all of the heavy metals and radio-active compounds that were naturally occurring in ground water. Then there were other contaminants like run off from industries and agricultural fields. The medical maladies caused by contaminated water was a feast for those who wanted to practice internal medicine, but it bore little relevance to surgery and didn't interest him. Finally, there was a lull in ER action, and he was able to consult with Dr. Yeager.

"Grandma Molly sure has a knack for opening worm cans," Debra Yeager said, "but she could be on to something. Never ignore a hunch from a devoted grandma, Dr. Jones. I have five grandchildren, and sometimes I observe things that their parents miss.

"Off the top of my head, I can tell you that both lead and arsenic are common well water contaminants around here, and both can cause colicky abdominal pain. I learned that from a family that kept using the ER for bellyaches. There are dozens of other potential contaminants and probably many that no one even suspects. And that's just in water. Then there are all of the toxins we all inhale, ingest and absorb from contaminated air, soil, food, clothing, carpeting, upholstery and mattresses. Our environment is a humungous witch's brew.

"What scares me is that no one really knows the long-term effects of the radiation we get from cell phones. The Farrells live in an affluent neighborhood, so they might already have a 5G tower radiating them. The energy waves from 5G are short distanced, so they have to put the cell towers up about every mile. How that radiation could affect humans, let alone fetuses and infants, hasn't really been studied. Toxicology is the ultimate detective game. Let's go talk to Grandma Molly about her concern.

"Oh, and on the subject of grandmas, beware the grandma caught in a mother-in-law triangle. Those grandmas always find fault with how the daughter-in-law is raising the child. In emergency medicine, it's truly important to consider the source of patient complaints. Parents, partners and children sometimes provide better clues than does the patient."

As Brody digested Dr. Debra's lessons, he thought about his own grandmothers, the one he dearly loved, and the one he hadn't seen since he was nine years old, after his father moved into loftier social circles. He wondered if his father was a badass because Grandma Jones was such a snooty bitch, unlike Grandma Molly who truly loved her grandkids.

Back in the suture room, Beryl was starting to stir, and Darryl was sleeping peacefully in Molly's lap. Dr. Yeager took over. "I understand you're concerned that something in the home water could be causing the baby's distress. It's a valid concern and we have a few options for looking into that. One is that the family can get their well water tested. There are home test kits on the market for common contaminants like lead. There are also independent laboratories that will do the testing. The city health department can also do some testing, but it can get costly to pin down a rare contaminant if the common ones aren't found.

"The second option is to test the baby. We'd need urine and blood samples to look for lead and arsenic, and the specimens would have to be sent to an outside reference lab. It could take some time to get results.

"A third option is to have Carol only mix the baby's formula with bottled water. However, it could take weeks to see if Darryl's symptoms improve after elimination of the well water, but gradual improvement might also mean she's outgrowing her colic.

"For the sake of time, testing Darryl would probably be the most expedient way to answer your question. If you want to sign the baby in, we can do the blood draw and try to catch a urine sample here and now, or the baby's pediatrician could do that, and then there wouldn't be any charges for an ER visit. However, if there's no evidence of lead or arsenic, then we'd have to refer you to a toxicologist to look into all of the other possible contaminates."

Molly said, "I've been thinking about this. Carol drinks a lot of tea, so she consumes plenty of water too. Wouldn't she also show signs of toxicity if the water's contaminated?"

"Not necessarily," Dr. Debra said. "Proportional to body size, the bigger person will have lower levels of the toxin in their system than the smaller one, even if they ingest a greater amount. The real danger though, is that the developing systems of young children are more vulnerable to toxins, especially with substances that are toxic to the nervous system."

"Let me talk to Carol about this," Molly responded. "At the moment, I think I need to get both of these kids home, if Beryl's okay to be discharged. It's been a long day."

Chapter Twenty-One

*D*ewy's next shift proved even more challenging than the bus crash shift. Rainy days usually meant more traffic accidents, and with CityStar Hospital being right near a major highway intersection, the ER was exceptionally busy.

Dewy would soon learn on this steamy summer day, characterized by periods of intense lightning and thunder, that storms were also associated with more animal bites. The reason for the animal anxiety was still being debated.

Shortly before the first cloudburst, an eighty-two-year-old man showed up with ragged wounds on his calf and shin. He had just exited a grocery store when a mangy mutt appeared out of nowhere and started chewing on his leg. He was able to defend himself by throwing a can of soup at the dog, which ran swiftly out of sight. Animal control was contacted, but even after the bitten man had been taken care of, the offending 'medium sized, scruffy, tan dog' had not been found.

Protocol dictated that the victim needed to be given the first two of the five shots he would need to prevent rabies, but for no good reason other than suspected greed on the part of the manufacturer, there was a nation-wide shortage of rabies vaccine. Dr. Patel referred the elderly victim to the health department so that state and federal authorities could determine if he was high enough risk to receive some of the rationed supply.

Just after the grocery shopper arrived, a Korean-speaking woman named Minji was checked in for a dog bite. She was taking a package out of her car trunk in her driveway when a neighbor walked by with his dog on a leash. The big dog pulled its leash out of its owner's hand and took a crushing bite out of Minji's backside. The dog was reportedly vaccinated, and Minji didn't want to notify animal control, because she didn't want to have any problems with her neighbor, who swore the dog had never previously bitten anyone.

Dewy now knew that state law required doctors to report any animal bite that needed medical attention. When she explained that to Minji, she was met with tears. The woman told Dewy of some of the difficulties she had with this particular neighbor, with whom she couldn't communicate due to her limited English. She begged Dewy to not report the bite.

"But what if this dog bites someone else?" Dewy argued. "And if your neighbor is that much of a scoundrel, how do we know for sure that the dog really is vaccinated, unless animal control checks its vet records? How do we know the dog never bit anyone else?

"What if it's true that the dog never bit anyone before, but it bit you today because it has rabies, because a rabid skunk bit it? We don't even have any rabies vaccine available if you've been exposed, but how do we know if you were exposed if the authorities don't check out the dog? Maybe, if the last time the dog bit someone, it had been properly reported, then you wouldn't be here now with a sore butt and a big hospital bill."

"What will happen if it's reported?" Minji asked.

"In this state, even healthy, vaccinated pets need to be quarantined for ten days for a serious bite. If the dog is unvaccinated or unhealthy, it could be euthanized or quarantine for six months."

Minji reiterated how fearful she was of this obnoxious neighbor, and Dewy found herself conflicted. She sought a consult with Dr. Patel.

"It absolutely has to be reported," he insisted. Nurse Hana called animal control and when the address was crosschecked, a previous dog bite report was found. Dewy shared that information with Minji.

"So, someone's going to go to my neighbor's house and take that dog away?" Minji asked. She became severely distressed when Dewy said yes. "I can't even go home now. That neighbor is going to take revenge on me. This is not fair; I will be a victim twice."

Dewy understood that the woman's language barrier made her uninclined to seek help from the police or a social worker. Dewy was upset by her inability to assist this victim as a physician. She could be more helpful if she was serving as a translator. Her ER experience seemed to be all about giving bad news to already stressed out people. She imagined psychiatry might be worse.

No sooner had she discharged Minji, a nine-year-old boy named Sam presented for a dog bite to his face by his own cocker spaniel. "Taffy is such a sweet dog," Sam's mother said. "She's never bit anyone ever, but she goes crazy when there's thunder. She gets frantic and Sammy was just trying to comfort her. It had to be an accident. She'd never hurt the kids. She was just scared. She's a sweet, gentle dog."

Sammy did better with his wound care than he did with the news about animal control. Both he and his mother became distraught. Just before she discharged them, Dewy overheard the mother telling Sam that they'd take Taffy to stay with relatives in another state. Dewy wondered how far the tentacles of the animal control authorities could reach.

Dr. Patel saw a pregnant woman who had been bitten by a raccoon. She had gone to throw her garbage out in the condo dumpster when her eyeglasses fell off of the top of her head and landed on a plastic bag. When she reached in to retrieve the glasses, the animal popped out from under some orange peels and bit her hand, damaging tendons. She couldn't bend her fingers and she needed urgent surgery. Then they'd have to hope the authorities would grant her access to rabies protection, unless animal control managed to catch the raccoon. Dewy wondered how they'd factor her pregnancy into their decision.

On top of the animal bites came the fire. A half-dead tree in front of an old clapboard house with boarded up windows was struck by lightning. The fire quickly sparked from the dead branches to the roof of the building, where inside, a dozen Chinese women slaved away at sewing machines, seven days a week, making sexy nightgowns out of cheap fabrics.

All of the women except one managed to escape before the entire building burst into flames. In addition to being hysterical about the one who didn't make it out, the women had all suffered smoke inhalation. Before they were able to break down the locked rear door by repeatedly bashing it with chairs, they got seriously dosed with the fumes of smoldering synthetic materials.

The fire department and five ambulance services had started administering oxygen to the victims on site, but most of the women were still coughing violently and having difficulty breathing. Respiratory therapists were pulled to the ER from all over the hospital, and Dewy wound up being the interpreter for all of the patients. With the help of a victim who spoke both Mandarin and Cantonese, Dewy also wound up translating the women's harrowing stories of sweatshop slavery for the investigating police.

Just when she was sure that things couldn't possibly get more insane, Xray informed Dewy that Molly Hudson was in the waiting room with the crybaby. This is too crazy, *c'est fou*, she thought in French.

When Dewy entered room seven, Darryl was sitting on the exam table, sucking on the fingers of one hand and holding a fuzzy toy in the other, which she would occasionally wave and shake. Except that she didn't smile, she looked like a normal healthy baby, perhaps a precocious baby, already sitting independently. Grandma Molly stood beside her.

"Hi Dr. Meadows," Molly said nervously, and then in almost a whisper, "Carol doesn't know I'm here. It's parents' day at the kids' camp, so she's there all day today, and I'm babysitting Darryl who's frantically teething. She's mouthing everything and being generally unhappy, in addition to her screaming fits; but that's not why I'm here today. I'm here for this."

Molly shone her phone light on Darryl's ear and Dewy saw that it looked red and puffy. When she looked closely, she saw some little marks on the earlobe. She looked with a magnifying lens and could distinguish almost closed-up puncture wounds. Darryl obviously didn't like her ear being touched and it felt warm. Dewy and Molly nodded to each other.

"I know cat bites are bad," Molly said, "and they need to be treated promptly with antibiotics. Terrell had a cat bite on his hand when he was five and he wound up in the hospital for almost a week before they got the infection under control. I can't imagine Carol saw this and ignored it, but I don't really know. When cat issues arise, I'm afraid my daughter tends to stick her head in the sand, or should I say, the kitty litter?"

As Dewy stifled a guffaw, she wondered how many other cat-related medical events the Farrell kids had suffered. What she knew about cat bites and the external ear made the baby's situation dangerous. As a medical student, Dewy had witnessed the case of a teenager with an infected bug bite on the back of his ear. The kid showed up a day too late. Ear cartilage was especially vulnerable to infection, and pus had eaten the ear up overnight, making it look like a piece of cauliflower. The infection required surgical drainage and the ear would eventually need plastic surgery to look less deformed. Not knowing when the baby had been bitten made this situation urgent.

Earlier that shift, Dr. Patel had reviewed animal bite management with the staff when the second dog bite showed up. He'd said that human bites were the dirtiest, but that the small sharp teeth of cats tended to deposit germs deep below the surface of innocent looking wounds. Cat bites needed to be managed with immediate antibiotic prophylaxis and careful monitoring. Dewy consulted with Dr. Patel about the baby, and he wanted to see the ear. He seemed to have a special interest in cat bites.

"Hello Molly," he said upon entering the room. They obviously knew one another but their greetings seemed awkward. "So, this is our little colicky baby. She's very cute." He carefully examined Darryl, and checked her all over for scratches, bites or swollen glands. Then he and Dewy stepped out of the room.

"Start intravenous antibiotics immediately. They penetrate cartilage much faster than oral medicine, and you cannot risk this fussy baby spitting out oral antibiotics that taste like crap. Tell pharmacy that this is an emergency and start warm compresses. The nurses will hate you for it, but it will get the antibiotic into the infected tissue faster. Get a picture of the ear and watch it closely, and we'll see where things are going over the course of our shift.

"And tell Grandma Molly we'll have to report this to animal control. How they'll ever figure out which kitty did it, I don't know. Maybe Harold Farrell can make bite impressions of all the cats to single out the guilty party, not that Carol would likely do anything about it except to defend the cat. The craziest thing about our state laws is that animal control will almost always take a vicious dog out of the home, but very rarely will they remove a vicious cat. Go figure!

"Dr. Meadows, we have another consideration here regarding the Farrells. In many ERs, child protective services would be called in to evaluate this situation for possible neglect. You'd better start thinking about whether or not this infant is at increased risk because of the situation in that home."

Dewy was dumbstruck by Dr. Patel's remarks. "Are you saying the authorities won't take the cats away, but they might take the children away?"

"I'm saying it's our job to use whatever resources we have to protect at-risk children. I suggest you consult Annette Durden in our social work department. Her office is now over at the children's hospital, but she's our liaison to child protective services and she can help you sort this out. I know you're very invested in this case, Dewy, but don't let your academic interest overshadow your duty to protect this baby from harm."

Baby Darryl's ear was already looking better when Dewy signed the case over to Dr. Brody Jones at the end of her shift. She told him she planned to consult with social services about the issue of reporting the case, and Brody would have to decide when it would be safe to switch to oral antibiotic and send the Farrells home.

When she got to her apartment, Dewy checked her Email. Her heart sank when there was still no response from Alex. It was so unlike him that she could not fathom the lack of communication. She treated herself to a glass of champagne, both to soothe herself and to celebrate managing to get out of the ER before the anticipated arrival of Carol Farrell. Then she drank another glass to toast Dr. Brody Jones for being the fall guy.

Chapter Twenty-Two

*O*n her day off from clinical duty, Dewy took a bus across town for her appointment with Social Service Director, Annette Durden at CMCH, CityStar Mothers' and Children's Hospital. The facility was as shiny and new as CityStar Hospital was old and dilapidated. Everything here seemed high-tech, from the architecture to the equipment, and the hallways were cheerful with children's art. Arriving ahead of schedule, Dewy took the opportunity to check the place out.

The ground floor housed the ER and specialty clinics. Another floor was for maternity patients and their healthy newborns. On another floor, an enormous neonatal intensive care unit served critically ill and premature babies transported from around the region. Another floor was divided into medical wards for infants, children and teens, and another floor was for surgical cases. The top floor included intensive care units and a ward for kids with cancer.

Dewy was unnerved by the sight of so many pale, bald little children trying to play, while simultaneously maneuvering around the IV poles that their chemo bags hung from. She hoped Gerald Farrell would not become one of them.

Dewy did a double take when she passed by a room where a few children were cuddling with a big black Labrador retriever. A nurse informed her that therapy animals could measurably reduce anxiety and depression in adult and pediatric cancer patients, and that the specially trained dog, named Kemosabe, and his owner visited the ward every day. The dog was considered a full-fledged member of the treatment team.

Dewy wondered how therapy animals might serve in a psychiatry practice. Like Zareen, her stepfather's gold-sniffing beagle, animals could have special talents.

Just before she entered Annette Durden's office, a young woman exited from it in tears. The office itself seemed well equipped for crying; there was a box of tissues on every surface. Sitting behind a sleek computer desk, Annette Durden was an imposing figure with a colossal afro hairdo. She appeared quite placid relative to the crying woman who had just walked out the door.

Dewy introduced herself and started to explain why she had made the appointment when Annette interrupted her. "Dr. Patel called me, so I know all about the return of the Farrells to CityStar's ER, the cat bite, and your interest in helping the baby."

"Did Dr. Patel also tell you about Merrill's facial injury and Gerald's cat scratch disease?"

"Yes, he did. It seems like you've started out your medical career in quite the puddle of quicksand, Dr. Meadows, and Dr. Patel is as worried about you as he is about the Farrell kids. He's had a high level of concern about those children for several years. So, what do you think you should do about reporting the Farrells to child protective services?"

"I'm here because I honestly don't know what to do, and Dr. Patel thought you could help me sort this out. He thinks the baby's cat bite warrants reporting this family for neglect, but I really struggle with that."

"Good for you, Dr. Meadows. I'm glad you struggle with that. I wish every doctor struggled before filing such a report. For every few families that are actually mistreating their children, and for each set of con artist parents who credibly stage accidents and literally get away with murdering their unwanted children, there is probably at least one hapless family that gets falsely accused.

"Last winter, we saw the case of a ten-month-old who had fallen out of his recliner onto blacktop. A doctor determined that the bleeding in his brain was too severe to have been caused by that fall, and other bruises on this baby made her suspect abuse. Consequently, all of the children were removed from the home. A few weeks later, another doctor identified a blood clotting disorder in this infant when he showed up in our ER with an unstoppable nosebleed. Even firm touch caused bleeding in his skin, and his loving parents were in no way responsible for his bruises.

"That family is now in therapy and in the court system, trying to repair the emotional and financial damages that were done to them by our very imperfect medical and social service systems. At least they might get justice, but I could spend hours telling you stories about devastated families that never recovered from the mistakes of well-meaning professionals.

"Let me tell you why Dr. Patel is right. He's right, because the law says that's what health care professionals must do. If you even think that a child is being neglected or abused, you need to report it and let the situation be investigated. If that child ultimately has a bad outcome, and records show that there were missed opportunities to rescue the child before they wound up gravely harmed or dead, whoever wrote those records could be liable. So, reporting your suspicions may not only save a child, but it could save you as well.

"Now, let me tell you why in this case, Dr. Patel is wrong. By the way, I suspect Dr. Patel sent you to me instead of making the decision about this himself, because if he instigated any action against the Farrells, it would become part of their lawsuits against him.

"What you need to know is that when we were dealing with Merrill's frequent ER visits for bellyaches, a social work student became very interested in the case, and like you, he was motivated to use his own time to check the Farrells out, even going so far as to visit Merrill's teachers. He also visited the Farrells in their home and at Harold's dental lab to get a better feel for them.

"We ultimately came to the conclusion that Carol Farrell is nuttier than a fruitcake, but she is not an abusive or a neglectful parent. If anything, she may be overly protective of her kids, except when it comes to the cats, and then, she's overly protective of the cats. She's not a warm loving mother, but if you overlook the cat issue, she is a very good caretaker.

"Are there too many cats in the house? Yes. Have the kids had problems because of the cats? Yes. But is that abuse or neglect? Should we take kids away because their parents are slobs, or they smoke weed, or play violent video games, or keep guns in their home?

"Every day in our ER, our doctors see children with fractures, lacerations, burns, head trauma, poisonings, and drownings, the vast majority of which are accidental. Sorting out which ones are not accidental is a complex process that starts with a health professional's gut feelings.

"Did that parent deliberately put Jilly in bath water that was too hot, or did Jilly turn the faucet on herself? Did Donald fall down the steps, or was he pushed? Was Dad negligent for leaving the power drill where Felix could play with it? What do we do about the family of a child who got into a cupboard and drank a fifth of tequila?

"Mom was on her phone when Cory fell in the pool and drowned. Should we now take her other kids away because records indicate she's on the phone a lot? All of our doctors see cell phone distraction as an important factor in childhood accidents. Even in the hospital, we see parents being inattentive to and detached from their children because they can't put their phones down. The definition of child neglect is a monstrous black hole.

"I'm going to let you in on some strictly confidential information. In my opinion, Dr. Patel has lost his objectivity regarding this family. He's an excellent doctor and he did everything appropriately when he was taking care of Merrill for his bellyaches, including arrangement of the psych consult that resulted in Merrill's hospitalization for the purpose of spying on the Farrells. Now, Carol has a defamation suit pending against him, in addition to the malpractice suit she has against all of the doctors who didn't diagnose Merrill's gallbladder parasite.

"I also suspect Dr. Patel's bias in this case might stem from his dislike of cats. He once told me that he's highly allergic to cats, and just being in a room with the Farrells made his eyes itch. We all have our biases, and we all have to live in a world full of allergens and irritants.

"I'm sure you know that as the ER attending, Dr. Patel is ultimately responsible for the decisions made by interns, and he is also directly responsible here, because he went in and saw the baby with you. You are both in a no-win situation. If the case is not reported and something worse happens to this baby, the two of you could be guilty of dereliction of duty.

"Think about it, Dr. Meadows. That baby will soon be able to crawl and get around. She, or any of the other kids in that family, could show up in the ER tomorrow with their entire face ripped to shreds by an irate cat that didn't like having its tail pulled.

"However, if you do report this and child protective services goes to investigate, Carol will probably start another lawsuit, and even though she probably won't win any of these lawsuits, they hang heavily over the heads of the doctors who are also incurring significant legal costs to defend themselves. As I understand the situation, the Farrells can afford top-notch attorneys, the kind that other lawyers don't like to do battle with; and the lawyers the malpractice carrier provides are sometimes more eager to settle the case than they are to defend the doctor. That forces the doctors to hire their own attorneys if they want to fight."

"So, what would you recommend I do?" Dewy asked.

"Dr. Meadows, here at Children's Hospital, just this week, our ER docs have reported three suspected cases of child abuse and neglect. Child Protection Services, a wholly underfunded and understaffed agency, has so far only been able to adequately follow-up on one of the cases, and the caseworker determined that this particular family is too dysfunctional to care for three kids under the age of five. However, as of this morning they still hadn't found a foster family to take those children together, so they're being split up, including a set of twins.

"So, you need to ask yourself this question: will the Farrell children be more at risk in their cat house, or in a dysfunctional foster care system? You need to do what is in the best interests of the children, even though there is risk with whatever you decide.

"There are legal, medical, social, psychologic, moral, and economic answers to your question, Dr. Meadows, but there is no right answer. I wish you luck with your decision."

Chapter Twenty-Three

"You've got to be kidding," Brody said, when Dewy told him about her meeting with Annette Durden. "It sounds like she made the decision even more difficult, or maybe we're just opening our eyes to how complicated this is. I could also be in a malpractice situation with the Farrells because of Merrill's drooping face. Do you think we need to hire lawyers for ourselves?"

It was their second dinner 'date' on a shared day off. Dewy was actually eager to have someone to talk to who really understood what her current life was like. Brody seemed to be about the only person in her small world who was unattached, and not eager to get home to a partner when he finished a shift, so their singularity seemed to be drawing them together.

In an intimate Italian restaurant, they commiserated about struggling to function as ER doctors. Brody liked the fast pace and the procedural experience, but not the interpersonal part. Dewy hated the fast pace. She wanted to communicate with and understand people, not do things to them.

Brody ordered an expensive bottle of brut champagne. "*Brut* means dry in French," Dewy said, but then she realized that Brody must have known that since that's what he ordered. Maybe he really did like champagne. Alex never did.

"I think I might go talk to the hospital lawyer about this. Since meeting with Annette Durden this morning, my head is just spinning, and I still don't know what to do.

"So, what did happen with Darryl's ear?" Dewy asked. "I felt so bad about dumping that one on you. When I first told Grandma Molly that we wanted to keep the baby for at least twelve hours, she tried to call Carol to tell her, but Carol didn't answer. Then I got tied up interpreting Mandarin for the internal medicine resident who had to admit one of the smoke inhalation victims, so I never did find out if and when Molly reached Carol. One of those poor fire victims was so bad they had to put her on a ventilator and admit her to ICU."

"Make that two," Brody said. "We were still doing breathing treatments on some of them when I left the ER this morning, and most were improving, but around three a.m., one of them dropped her oxygen so low that Dr. Olga had to put her on a ventilator. All of the victims that were still there this morning will have their airways scoped to see how bad the damage is. The ones who improved enough to be discharged were sent to a shelter. Hard to believe these situations exist here in America, and probably more often then we'll ever know."

"I saw the news about the fire when I got back from the children's hospital. One of those women told me that the owner of that factory smuggles the workers here with phony passports and visas and then takes their I.D. away. The women, who were seamstresses in China, thought they were being brought here to serve as nannies in affluent homes. They were truly enslaved in that firetrap, sleeping on cots in the basement, because it was too hot in the attic where the cots had originally been set up.

"According to the news, they were all illiterate, so they signed these indentured agreements that give them no legal recourse in their own country. The authorities think this thug has other factories. These poor women will probably all be deported once they are medically stable. The whole situation is just so horrible; I want to forget about it for now.

"Were you able to get any sleep today?" Dewy asked Brody, noticing he didn't have the under-eye shadows he usually sported when she'd see him at the end of a shift.

"After last night's shift, I slept like a baby all day. I should correct that. I slept all day, but poor Baby Darryl did not sleep so well. Around six a.m. she had one of her screaming fits and Carol was right there screaming with her that we needed to do something. We were going to give her a dose of morphine, but she stopped screaming before pharmacy sent it over.

"Grandma Molly apparently reached Carol just after you signed Darryl over to me. When I went to check on the baby, Molly told me that Carol was coming to the ER to be with Darryl, while she was headed to their house to babysit the rest of the grandkids. I was just dreading Carol's arrival, but she wasn't in her usual state of rage when she got there around eight. In fact, she was kind of on the defensive.

"I was really glad you took that close-up picture of the baby's ear before you started treatment, because by the time Carol got there, it was already looking better. As soon as I showed her the picture, she got kind of quiet, and then she showed me papers from her vet that said the new cat was healthy. Apparently when she got the call from Molly about the bite to Darryl's ear, Carol's first instinct was to run to the vet to get the kitten a health certificate.

"Carol said she was sure it was the new kitten that bit the baby because the kitten was drawn to the smell of the formula. She thinks the baby had spit up some of her feeding and Bilko probably 'accidentally' bit Darryl's ear when he was lapping up the spit up, which must have dribbled onto her ear.

"Carol swore that none of the other cats would do a thing like that. She also swore that she would make sure that it would never happen again, though I have no idea what she can do to prevent it. Stop feeding the baby? Put a clothespin on the cat's nose? Lock them all up? I really can't imagine what it's like in that house full of kids and cats and that screaming baby. The screaming really is pitiful. I will forever be sympathetic to the parents of colicky infants.

"Anyway, when I rounded this morning with the second-year resident, the ear looked good, the third dose of IV antibiotic was on board, and Carol was chomping at the bit to go home, so we discharged Darryl on oral antibiotics. I have no doubt that Carol will administer them religiously and she'll return if the ear puffs up again."

"Did you ask her about the other kids?"

"I didn't have to. Once I finished telling her about the baby's treatment, she gave me the lowdown. Beryl is struggling with her right hand in a splint, but the other kids at camp have been helping her. Gerald had a needle biopsy of the big lymph node in the oncologist's office and they're waiting for the results, which they won't have until sometime next week. He's still acting like a miserably sick child. And, Merrill's face is a horrible mess, thanks to me, and they are seeing an oral surgeon on Monday.

"And, if you're interested, she's taking Bronco to the vet on Saturday because she noticed a lump on his rump, and Babo hasn't had any more seizures since they adjusted the dose of her seizure medicine. I made the mistake of showing Carol a picture of Hairy Potter, hoping she'd think better of me if I was also a cat person, and then she started to tell me about all of the cat's health problems. I don't think there's enough days in the week for the doctor, dentist, and the vet appointments this woman must have to keep up with, with seven kids and who knows how many cats.

"Hey, let's forget about the Farrells long enough to enjoy our dinner. I slept right through lunchtime and I'm starving." As he devoured his veal masala, Dewy picked at her eggplant parmesan. Brody asked her if she was okay.

"Just overwhelmed, Brody. Seeing those abused choking women all day yesterday, seeing all of those little kids with cancer today, and hearing Annette Durden talk about the horrible things that people do to their children, makes me acutely aware of how cruel a world we live in. Yet every other day, I'm questioning my decision to be a physician and spend my life trying to solve other people's problems. I could be an interpreter like my sister and be going to parties every night, instead of reading about lymphoma and arsenic poisoning. I'm starting to wonder why I'm doing this to myself. Do you ever feel that way?"

"Dewy Silver Tongue, I'm truly sorry you feel that way. I love what I'm doing. I don't love every part of it, but I know my dexterity was gifted to me for a reason, and I've known my whole life that I would be a sculptor of some variety. It started for me in the sandbox. My mother still has clay figures I made for her when I was in grade school. I worked with wood, stone and bronze in college, and I am pursuing my destiny to sculpt humans.

"What I want to know is; why aren't you taking your linguistic ability to a more rewarding career? Why aren't you working for the CIA as an international spy? You don't really like blood and guts, and you say you love figuring people out, and you obviously like solving mysteries. Didn't you ever think about becoming a secret agent?"

Dewy answered with a Mandarin accent. "How you know I not Chinese national, here to steal American medical trade secrets?"

Did she wink at him when she said that? Brody wasn't sure.

She reverted to perfect English. "So, tell me how you know about the restaurant scene in this big city."

"I have a high school buddy who went to culinary school here while I was in college. He's never given me a bad recommendation. I'll get a reservation at a Korean restaurant tomorrow night, if you'll join me."

"Love to, if you let me pay my own way."

Chapter Twenty-Four

*D*r. Brody Jones was enjoying a disaster-free shift. It was a pretty summer day and most of the patients showing up in the ER weren't there for illness. There was the usual assortment of injuries, sprinkled with an occasional wheezer or infected bug bite. A lawn service employee who disturbed a wasp's nest was in serious condition after incurring multiple stings.

The most frustrating case Brody had seen the whole day was a man who had been trying to pass a kidney stone for a week. An ultrasound exam showed the stone was too big to pass; it was stuck in a swollen ureter. They were waiting for a urologist to take him to an OR and snake a catheter in there to blast the stone with a laser beam, scoop out the pieces with a basket, and vacuum up the dust. Brody thought that urologists had some of the coolest surgical tools. The kidney stone patient was in agony, in spite of pain medication.

Brody was looking forward to signing his few stable patients over to the nightshift, when Xray informed him that Carol Farrell had just signed in for suture removal for Beryl's hand. Brody was fine with that, until Xray added that she had the whole family and the housekeeper with her. "She wants them all checked for manganese poisoning. Apparently, she had her well water tested and the results came back that there was a high manganese level. She tried to get it done in her doctor's office, but he didn't have the right kind of test tubes for the blood. Neither did an urgent care clinic, and they told her to come here."

"Wait a minute," Dr. Ted Schwartz said, before Xray handed the charts to Brody. "They can all get tested without us having to see them all. We only need one suspicious case to order the tests on all of them. Find out if there's one kid she's especially worried about, and let's start there. We can send the rest of them to the lab."

Dr. Ted Schwartz was the director of emergency medicine for CityStar Hospital. He had spent the last month supervising in the new ER at the new children's hospital, and it was his first day back at old CityStar since the new interns started in July. He'd met the interns during their orientation but hadn't yet worked with any of them. He was delighted to hear that Dr. Brody Jones was doing an excellent job and had even managed to ingratiate himself to Carol Farrell. He was distraught to find out that the Farrells were using his ER again, but relieved to know that with just a few hiccoughs, two of the interns had gained Carol's trust.

"Rumor has it that you speak cat, Dr. Jones. I guess that's what it takes to have Carol Farrell seeking you out as her personal physician. X says she called to ask who was on duty."

Brody wished he had never made that cat connection with Carol. Since he had, everyone on staff had wanted to see a picture of Hairy Potter.

Brody asked Dr. Schwartz if he had any experience with manganese toxicity.

"I know it's a brain problem. I once saw a welder with terrible tremors, like Parkinson's disease, which is what I thought it was until he said his coworkers in the canning factory were also shaky. Parkinson's isn't contagious, so we ultimately figured out that they all had manganese poisoning from breathing in the welding fumes.

That was a few decades ago and I haven't heard a word about manganese since."

Brody consulted a toxicology website. A natural and abundant earth element, manganese was considered an essential dietary mineral, important to numerous body functions. However, excessive manganese exposure could damage the nervous system, the heart and the liver. It had only recently been realized that excessive manganese exposure in young children could result in lower IQs, hyperactivity, poor coordination and oppositional behavior. Well water was often the source of manganese poisoning, and the Environmental Protection Agency didn't even regulate how much manganese was allowable in municipal water. Water safety governance was decades behind the science.

Brody gritted his teeth when he learned that Carol Farrell insisted on signing in Merrill, Gerald, and Darryl. Removing the sutures from Beryl's hand would turn out to be the easiest part of the visit.

The Farrells were stuffed into room six like sardines. Crowded onto the two exam tables and a single stool, sat three adults and two adolescents, each with a younger child in their lap. Carol introduced Dr. Brody Jones to Harold, a lanky angular figure with hair the color of paprika, coke bottle green eyes behind coke bottle thick eyeglasses, and beautiful teeth. After saying hello, Harold never said another word, nor did the elderly housekeeper, Tia Williams.

Brody was struck by the family resemblances and the exception. Cheryl, Merrill and the baby had Harold's coloring, while blonde Terrell, Gerald and Laurel had Carol's magnetic baby-blues. Most strikingly, Beryl looked different than all of them. With turquoise eyes and caramel coloring, Brody thought Beryl would be truly gorgeous if she could just be relieved of Harold's beaky nose. She didn't flinch at all when Brody removed her sutures, but then she complained that her hand was stiff, and she couldn't open it. Nurse Hana wrapped her hand in a microwaved heat-pack for a few minutes and then helped her to stretch away the stiffness.

Merrill's face looked slightly less droopy, and Brody asked Carol how he was doing with eating and drinking.

"Not good. We took him to see Dr. Patrick, an oral surgeon who uses Harold's dental lab. Dr. Patrick says Merrill has Bell's palsy, and that the droop is temporary. He started him on steroids to speed up recovery. He said that for the whole side of his face to droop like that, the nerve would have to have been traumatized up here, by his temple, not down by his mouth. He told us that sometimes the nerve that controls the facial muscles goes weak because of a viral infection, and sometimes it goes nuts for no good reason; but in Merrill's case it was probably the trauma that caused Bell's palsy. We're still going to take him to the neurosurgeon for another opinion, but we think he's already improving.

"Dr. Patrick also said you did a gorgeous job of repairing his lips. You've redeemed yourself, Dr. Jones."

Brody pulled up the picture of Merrill taken on his last visit, and he could see the improvement too. He was so relieved that he wasn't going to get sued for damaging this kid's face, that his psyche felt fifty pounds lighter.

"So, tell me about the manganese problem. I confess, it's not something I learned about in med school."

"I am very worried about this," Carol said. "We've had our well water checked every year since we live in this house, but now I've learned that the testing company was only checking for bacteria and what they call 'primary contaminants' like lead and arsenic. I called the testing company and asked if there's anything else they've found in well water around our part of town, and the guy told me that some wells have shown high manganese levels.

"Apparently, there are primary and secondary contaminants, and the Environmental Protection Agency only regulates the primaries. Manganese is a secondary contaminant, so the testing company didn't bother to test for it, even though they knew it could be a problem in our neighborhood. We've since learned that our subdivision used to be an agricultural field that got sprayed with pesticide, which could be the source of the manganese.

"The test showed that our well water has more than twice the amount of manganese considered safe for human consumption. The bastards knew about this, and they never told us about it or did that test in their yearly analyses."

Uh-oh, went Brody's brain; another lawsuit on the horizon.

"I've read all about manganese toxicity," Carol continued. "I didn't read that it causes pain, but it causes irritability, and young infants are especially vulnerable to toxicity. Did you know, that infant formulas are extremely high in manganese, and soy-based infant formulas are even higher, Dr. Jones? I don't know if that's what makes Darryl cry all the time, but this poor baby has been getting extra doses of manganese in every goddamn feeding since I stopped nursing her. So please test her for manganese poisoning."

"And she never smiles," big sister Cheryl added. "She's just not a happy baby like my little sisters were."

"Yeah," agreed Terrell. "I could make my other baby sisters laugh, but Darryl just looks at me like I'm a doofus."

"That's because you are a doofus," Merrill sputtered.

"You're a dork." Terrell retorted.

"That's enough!" Carol barked and the kids immediately buttoned up.

"I want Merrill tested because he doesn't have a gallbladder, and the website said that the liver and gallbladder are the organs that help get rid of excess manganese. Also, Merrill came home from neonatal intensive care on a soy-based formula that I mixed with tap water. Except for Merrill and Darryl, all the other kids were breast-fed, but Gerald also wound up on formula. I stopped breast-feeding him early because I got put on medication for post-partum depression. You know, as soon as those pregnancy hormones take a dive, I get really depressed. Usually I can fight the blues, but that time I couldn't."

"But that's when Banjo died, Mommy. Remember?" Cheryl interjected. "Banjo was a nice old kitty," the teenager explained to Dr. Jones.

Carol shot her daughter a silencing look and turned back to Brody. "Banjo was my cat since college. She was a stray when I adopted her, and she was a wonderful cat. I still miss that kitty," she lamented, and then she quickly snapped back to a less nostalgic state.

"I am most worried about Gerald because he has the symptoms of manganese poisoning. Gerald is not showing his academic potential, and he's on medication for hyperactivity; except he's off it now, because he's lethargic from the lymph node infection. We got the biopsy results. It's not cancer, so we just have to wait this damn cat scratch thing out."

"And you have to get rid of Bluto," Gerald added. "He scratched me and made me sick. He's a bad kitty. He hisses and he scratches."

"Bluto won't scratch you, Gerald, if you just leave him alone. Bluto only has one eye and he can't tell when he's too close to you, so you just have to stay away from him. He didn't mean to hurt you.

He's just an old, half-blind kitty and you need to be calm when you're around him because he scares easily." Carol turned back to Brody.

"Bluto had a tumor on his eye, and it was malignant. They had to take his eye out last year, so now he's kind of a nervous boy, poor old cat. He's usually very tolerant of the children, but Gerald can get very wound up and the cats get a little skittish around him sometimes. You know how cats are."

Brody could only shake his head affirmatively as Carol continued.

"And, I want to be tested because pregnancy increases absorption of manganese, and I drink a lot of tea and eat a lot of nuts, both of which are high in manganese. And, I want Tia our housekeeper tested, because older people may be more sensitive to manganese and Tia also drinks a lot of tea. And I want the rest of us tested because we've been living in that house for eleven years, and not only can you eat and drink manganese, but you can inhale it from the steam in your shower.

"And, I want all of our medical problems well documented so I can sue the damn water testing bastards for not telling us about manganese when they found out about it. Damn idiots! They could have made more money if they told people about it and tested for it, and maybe my family wouldn't be having all of these damn problems.

"I'm going to sue the city health department too. They put out these recommendations about how you need to get your well water tested annually, and there's not one mention of manganese on their website. Why aren't they telling people about this? Damn idiot bastards are poisoning my family."

The litigious Carol Farrell made Brody sweat. He dutifully wrote scripts for all ten people to take to the lab to have their manganese levels checked. He stayed on after the end of his shift to check out the education he had just received from the crazy cat lady. It was actually pretty interesting stuff.

He wondered if manganese poisoning could be why his sister's elementary school students seemed to all be cranky and hyper. His sister Jody was an art teacher in a rural school district, and she had repeatedly commented to Brody about many of her pupils being over-active and ornery. She taught in an agricultural community, where maybe everyone's well water was contaminated with pesticides.

Brody methodically wrote-up the visit information to document Carol's concerns. He couldn't wait to tell Dewy. Maybe this was the answer to the baby's problem. He had new respect for Molly Hudson and for the wisdom of a loving grandmother.

Chapter Twenty-Five

"**W**hich do you want first, the good news or the bad news?" Brody asked Dewy as they settled into the cozy cushioned booth of an Indian restaurant for a late dinner. Dewy had had the day off and Brody had finally finished his dayshift. The restaurant was posh and exotic and Dewy's eyes almost fell out of her head when she saw the prices on the menu.

"Start with the good news."

"No cancer on Gerald Farrell's lymph node biopsy, and Merrill's droopy face has been diagnosed as Bell's palsy, and he's already improving on prednisone."

"What a relief," *eot-teon guho*, she thought in Korean. "That's great news, Brody, for you and for the kids. "How do you know that?"

Brody told her about the visit and the whole manganese thing, and Dewy's jaw dropped.

"There must be some reason the Farrells came into my life. You're not going to believe this, Brody, but I've heard about manganese poisoning. A few years ago, my stepdad was doing a consult for an expanding manganese mine in the Ukraine, and he was at a meeting where the local authorities wanted the mine owner to explain how they were going to protect the children living near the mine.

"Daddy Dave brought home a research paper for his boss about neurologic deficits in children living in that community. The paper was in Russian and my mother translated it into English and told me about it. Apparently, there are a lot of troubled kids living near that mine. I hope that's not what's affecting the Farrell kids because the brain damage is irreversible."

"Only you, Dewy, seem to know about these weird things that no one else has ever heard of. Maybe you're supposed to be an ER doctor.

"Carol actually gave me a whole lecture on manganese poisoning from stuff she read. She's no dummy, that crazy cat lady. Then, I read more about it when I went to write up my notes. There's data coming out of Brazil about kids being neurologically damaged by manganese in the water, soil and the air near the mines. Maybe manganese poisoning is what makes Carol such an angry woman."

"Probably not. My department chairman, Dr. Ortiz, gave me the lowdown on Carol, and apparently, she's been a nut job her whole life. The husband is supposedly a strange bird too. He was an abandoned toddler in diapers, found wandering on a highway. An adoptive family raised him because no one ever claimed him. Can you imagine someone doing that to a child?"

"I met Harold," Brody said. "Carol wanted the whole family tested for manganese. She even brought the housekeeper with her. Harold's a very quiet man who could benefit from a less prominent nose and a stronger jaw. I wonder if he ever gets to say a word in that household.

"Meanwhile, Carol's already changed their drinking water to bottled water, and she's having a reverse osmosis filtration system installed in the whole house. She's also hired an environmental lawyer to go after the health department and the water testing company for not putting out notices about the high levels of manganese in some wells.

"If a businessperson had ten Carol Farrells working for them, they could conceivably rule the world. For all of her craziness, she's actually a pretty high-functioning person.

"I think I also got a flash of insight about Carol's having so many kids. She said something about how depressed she gets when the pregnancy hormones decline, and I wonder if she keeps getting pregnant to avoid depression. I've never heard of anything like that, but hormones do make humans do crazy things."

"That's a really interesting theory. I need to look into that.

"Brody, I'm really glad to hear the good news about Gerald and Merrill, but I'm still worried about that baby. If it turns out that Darryl has a high level of manganese, does that mean we can stop looking for some other source of pain? Is being ornery the same thing as being in pain?"

"Well, who's still looking? I thought it was colic and she'll outgrow it."

Dewy pouted. "I guess I'm the only one who still thinks there's something else going on. I know everyone else thinks she's just a colicky baby with an over-reactive mother, but I can't shake the feeling that there's something really wrong, something that we're all missing. It keeps gnawing at me."

"Did you decide what to do about reporting them to child protective service for the cat bite? I wonder if manganese in the water could make the cats ornery."

"I didn't, and that's eating at me too. My instincts tell me that Carol is right; that there's something going on with Darryl beyond colic, and I just do not believe that she is a neglectful mother, even if she's not the most loving of mothers. I don't think I'm going to file that report."

"Then trust your instincts Dewy. You seem to have really good instincts. So, what do your instincts say about coming home with me after dinner? I know this sounds like a really lame pickup line, but I'd like to show you my art and I have a really nice bottle of champagne in the fridge."

Chapter Twenty-Six

When Brody pushed the top button on the elevator panel of the luxurious hi-rise, Dewy figured her new friend must come from some serious money. Even then, she could not have anticipated the opulence of Brody's digs. With spacious rooms including two bedroom suites, an art studio, high ceilings full of skylights, and a wraparound balcony that overlooked the city skyline, Dewy could hardly believe her surroundings. Nor could she believe the sculptures, pottery, paintings, and unique art that decorated the place. When Brody took a bottle of Dom Perignon out of the beverage fridge in his gourmet kitchen, Dewy thought she must be in a dream. She immediately started to fantasize about being his roommate in the second bedroom.

With the magnificent Hairy Potter sitting in his lap, Baby Face Brody and Silver Tongue Dewy sat on the balcony and toasted the orange smear that was the last vestige of an August sunset. "So, you've heard my story, Dr. Jones. Tell me more about yourself and your art, and how you can afford to live like this on an intern's salary."

Brody laughed. "I can't, but Daddy's got a guilt complex. He never took care of our family emotionally, but he tries to make up for that by taking care of us financially. I was so angry with my father for most of my youth that I didn't want to be anything like him, and when I started college, I started out as an art major.

"I was a freshman when one of my professors befriended me, and I started hanging out with him. It didn't take me long to realize that this talented guy was basically poor. He worked really hard at his art and made museum quality bronzes, but if he didn't have a teaching job, he wouldn't be able to feed himself. I looked at his life and I looked at my family's life, and that's when I switched to a pre-med curriculum.

"Here's the math, Dewy. My father does about sixteen procedures a week: noses, facelifts, boobs, tummy tucks, and the like, and he makes between ten and twenty thousand dollars on each procedure. He also does about that many consults a week, for which people pay five hundred dollars out of pocket. It's all cash; no insurance.

"I wish I could tell you about all of the famous people whose faces he's redesigned. He doesn't create those little ski-slope noses that some plastic surgeons sculpt for everyone. My father creates uniquely beautiful noses that harmoniously blend with people's faces. That's why he's so successful. His income easily exceeds a million a year from his practice, he only works four days a week, and he takes time off whenever he feels like it. On top of that, he has an A-team financial advisor and he makes millions with his investment portfolio.

"He bought this condo for me. To him, it's just another investment. He'll probably make a million when he sells it at the end of my surgical residency, five years from now. So, while I don't want to be like him, I've come to appreciate that my skills have a loftier purpose than those of my art professor; not only because I'll have good earnings, but because I can help people, and not just the beautiful people. I can help people with cleft lip, and people whose faces have been disfigured by trauma or burns."

After refilling their champagne glasses, Brody beckoned Dewy off of the balcony to give her a tour. One whole wall had comic illustrations drawn by his mother, in which the feature character was a cat. Another wall contained watercolor portraits by his mother of famous comedians. Another wall had shelves upon which sat playful cat figures, carved out of wood and stone. There were also ceramic planters with unique inlaid mosaics in which exotic plants flourished. There were numerous sketches and carvings in progress in the art studio.

Dewy was totally impressed by the library of surgical textbooks in the living room loft, accessed by a spiral staircase. The fabulous kitchen smelled of recent spicy cooking. Brody showed her the art in the two inviting bedroom suites without ever motioning towards the bed. It was all so incongruous with the macho man that she had come to know in the ER.

They returned to the balcony to enjoy the cool of the evening. "Did your mother remarry after your father split?" Dewy asked, increasingly intrigued by Dr. Brody Jones.

"My mom has had a significant other for years, but they maintain separate homes because if she did remarry or live with Gordon, she'd no longer receive alimony from my father. It's her revenge, and my father can well afford it. She's probably better off not living with Gordon anyway, because she's such a free spirit."

"How so?" Dewy wanted to know.

"My mom, Josie; can you believe Josephine Sorenson married Joseph Jones to become Josie Jones? Then, Josie Jones and Nosy Jones named my sister Jody Jones. I was lucky to get by with Brody. Your mother and Carol Farrell aren't the only ones guilty of ritualistic naming.

"So anyway, my mom Josie is really the artist in the family. She started out as a cartoonist for Disney. When they went all digital, she moved into mixed media, and one of my father's patients, a movie director, hired her as a set designer. She did a lot of famous movie scenes, but she stopped doing that after Jody was born. Later on, with her stellar credentials she went freelance. Currently, she does occasional movie sets, book illustrations, and she loves to do caricatures for corporate events. At the parties, she gets to eat, drink and draw silly pictures of people, and come home with a thousand dollars, but it's only an occasional gig. I'm thinking that she's busy in her home studio, creating masterpieces every day, instead of keeping house for a domestic partner."

"So, you and your mom and dad must all look at faces and think of how you'd redo them. I have a sister who looks at people and all she can think about is how she would redesign their attire. How would you redo my face?" Dewy asked. "I'm serious and I'm truly curious."

Brody envisioned Dewy with fuller lips and some eyebrow lift, but her facial structure and features were otherwise very attractive, and her complexion was glowingly gorgeous. She wouldn't even need surgery, just some collagen to her lips and Botox to her forehead. She was adorable with her dark chocolate brown, boyish haircut, but he envisioned her with much sexier hair to go with her sexy scrubs. It was odd how her scrubs were more seductive than the casual, conservative clothes she wore outside of the hospital. "I'd never fix what isn't broken," Brody said, hoping he sounded sincere.

Dewy didn't believe him. She thought he was being kind. "Why don't you have a girlfriend, Dr. Brody Jones, or do you have many?"

"Been there, done that" Brody said with some hubris. "Back in college, I was this beardless art major and I had to prove I was macho man. I had numerous girlfriends until I got serious about going to med school. Then, I became devoted to studying, and between my art and having to do a lot of catch up education, I just put dating on hold. Even in med school, I had friends who I studied with and friends who I dined with, but then as now, I want to keep it noncommittal. I am currently married to my goals.

"What about you, Dewy? Why aren't you in a relationship? Is it just the student thing? You also seem like a super serious student, which is refreshing. Half of the surgical residents I've met in my program strike me as shallow, self-loving opportunists like my father."

Dewy was blown away by Brody's description of their fellow resident physicians. She also felt like at least half of the medical students she had met along the way were going into medicine for the wrong reasons. For so many students, it seemed like their smarts and their family expectations had pushed them into medical school, but they weren't motivated to help people. They were there because it was the lucrative or narcissistic thing to do. She wasn't entirely sure about her own motivations.

"I'm a transient, Brody. My father and stepfather moved our family around my whole life, and I've moved around in my adult life between my parents' homes, college, med school, and now I'm in this city for my internship, but I don't know where I'll be next. It's hard to settle into a relationship when you know you're going to be moving on, but I do appreciate your friendship, Brody. It's nice to have a friend who understands that commitment is not what I'm looking for. I've had lots of friends in the course of my transient life, but then they turn out to be situational companions because I keep moving on."

Surely that was what her relationship with Alex had turned out to be. She expected to get a Dear Dewy email any day, if Alex would even be kind enough to tell her it was over.

Maybe Brody would become a good friend. He was certainly an interesting character.

Chapter Twenty-Seven

It was the first time that Dewy had worked with ER Director, Dr. Ted Schwartz, and she was in awe of him. The man seemed to have the ability to watch over everything going on in the entire ER, while simultaneously taking care of his own patients. Dewy couldn't fathom how anyone could do that. During a few moments of downtime, Liselle Grady gave her his story.

"Dr. Ted was a commanding medical officer during the Gulf War. He managed a ward full of soldiers mutilated by roadside bombs, and he also became an expert in 'Gulf War Syndrome.' Now the government calls it 'chronic multi-symptom illness', but the name change doesn't alter the condition that affects almost a third of the soldiers who saw combat in that war in 1990-91. We're talking about a quarter of a million men and women suffering from fatigue, headaches, memory problems, digestive issues, rashes, and other nasty stuff, and a third of them wind up with lethal tumors. My little brother Miguel was one of the soldiers who worked on the burning oil fields. He wound up with lung cancer and he's long gone. Dr. Schwartz still occasionally identifies a patient with this syndrome, even three decades later.

"After the Gulf War, Dr. Ted specialized in cardiovascular surgery. Maybe he was one of the best in the country; but after two decades, the development of arthritis in his hands caused him to transfer to emergency medicine. He can still sew up lacerations like they're child's play, but he can no longer tolerate the sustained hand steadiness it takes to delicately scrape a tumor off of a carotid artery.

"We are truly fortunate to have him here. I think the only reason he's still working at old CityStar, is that his elderly mother resides in a nearby nursing home. I just wonder where our esteemed Dr. Schwartz might wind up when his mother no longer binds him to this city. There are more prestigious hospital systems in prettier places than here, and Dr. Ted has the vitality of a man half his age. He does limp a little from a war wound though."

Dewy was anxious to run the case of the Farrell baby by this experienced doctor to see if he had any new ideas. That opportunity never came. Before Dewy even got to approach Dr. Ted, an ambulance arrived, bearing victims of a mass shooting in a nearby restaurant.

The shooter was a disgruntled chef who had recently been fired from his long-time job at the popular eatery, because he had become prone to sloppy performance and drunken tirades. He staged his attack at the peak of the dinner hour when two-dozen people were waiting for a table in an overcrowded foyer. Wearing chef's garb, he strode through the crowd, through the dining room and into the kitchen. Once there, he pulled a semi-automatic rifle out from behind his apron and shot three workers, while others took cover. Then he shot a bunch of appliances, grabbed a waitress as a hostage, went back into the dining room, and fired off multiple rounds as people scrambled to get out the door or under a table.

The siege ended when two kitchen workers managed to get behind him. One threw hot oil on him, while the other hit him in the head with a skillet and stabbed him with a butcher's knife. Multiple patrons joined in the fray to subdue him, and the gun fired more rounds in the confusion. It was all over in less than ninety seconds.

By the time the ambulances arrived, there were four dead, nineteen people with gunshot wounds, and a dozen or more who were injured trying to get out of harm's way. The shooter had serious burns and the hostage waitress had splash burns. The most critical patients wound up in the CityStar ER, along with police, reporters and the victims' dining partners, some of who were wearing their meal. The whole place smelled of wine and garlic.

Dr. Ted was working to stabilize the shooter. The knife wound wasn't fatal, but when they cut away his oil-soaked clothes, his back was severely burned.

Liselle Grady was working the backup call list, seeking all of the general and specialty surgeons she could manage to recruit. Most of the victims had been shot in the back as they tried to get away, but ricocheting bullets had also hit people in other body parts. A kitchen worker with a bullet in his liver couldn't be transfused fast enough to keep up with the blood loss. In spite of heroic effort, the code team couldn't save him.

An eleven-year-old boy whose father took a fatal bullet to shield him was uninjured, but mute from shock. The boy's mother was one of the critical cases on her way to surgery. Dewy didn't envy the second-year psych resident who got assigned to help the youngster cope with his impending orphanhood.

Dewy got more experience inserting chest tubes than she could ever want. People shot in the back tended to have collapsed lungs if not severed spines and exploded kidneys.

She stabilized a devastated young man who had just been hired by the philharmonic. He was a violinist with a shattered forearm, though the arm had deflected the bullet that would otherwise have hit his head.

She tried to comfort a seventeen-year-old girl who had a bullet lodged in her neck. The young woman was a competitive gymnast at risk of becoming quadriplegic. She would be the second neuro-surgery case; the first was a kitchen worker who took a bullet to the head. The wait was unbearable for the young woman who was restrained so that she couldn't move. Even a sneeze could make the bullet scrape her spinal cord.

Dr. Schwartz got into a loud confrontation with a policeman who wanted the shooter to get priority treatment so he would live to face justice. Dr. Ted argued that there were others with more critical problems. CityStar Hospital only had ten operating rooms, and the shooter, who needed extensive debridement of burned skin, would just have to wait his turn. "Take him to another hospital if you think they can give him faster care."

Dr. Schwartz had to call the policeman's superior before the issue was resolved. He also had to keep giving updates to the press about the shooter's status. When the major networks showed up, one of the reporters noticed Dewy in her slinky silver scrubs. Dr. Ted observed the reporter chase her down with a camera until he had her cornered. "How is the staff holding up?" the journalist asked.

"To the kitchen workers who took down the gunman," Dewy said first in English and then in Spanish: "Your bravery and quick thinking saved many lives tonight. You are the heroes of this trag-edy. The ER staff grieves for and with the victims, the deceased, and their families."

Then she turned away and the reporter followed her to the room where she was treating the splash burns of the man who threw the hot oil on the shooter. The reporter was all excited to interview the hero, until he found out the man only spoke Spanish. Then he went looking for another eyewitness.

The shift finally ended and the last of the surgical cases were on their way to ORs. There had been no time to discuss anything with Dr. Schwartz except for the patients at hand. As they finished morning sign-outs, Dr. Ted confronted Dewy. "That was wonderful P.R. you did for CityStar Hospital. The administration is going to love it. That film clip will probably be their next TV ad. Congratulations, Dr. Meadows! I'd tell you to make sure you get compensated if they make you their poster girl, but your contract says they can do whatever they like with photos of residents performing their clinical duties." He grinned, "I must tell you though, you're getting a bit of a reputation as a black cloud doc."

"Black cloud?" Dewy knitted her brows.

"Well, come on, Dr. Meadows; children's bus crashes, illegal factory fires, mass food poisonings and mass shootings, and Carol Farrell, all in a few weeks' time. You'd think we were in a war zone. Old CityStar ER has probably never seen that much action compacted into one intern's rotation. Everyone likes you Dr. Meadows, but the nurses might just celebrate when your rotation ends. Let's hope the black cloud doesn't follow you to your next rotation. What is your next rotation, by the way?"

Dewy thought he was kidding, but she wasn't entirely sure. "Pediatrics is next."

"The black cloud isn't what we want for our pediatric community," Dr. Schwartz said, "but doctors who train under black clouds are much better trained doctors. That will be your silver lining, Dr. Dewy Silver Tongue."

Chapter Twenty-Eight

ER use was notoriously unpredictable, but the most predictably busy times were Sundays and Mondays in the late afternoon and evening. There were usually two physician assistants on duty on those shifts, but this Sunday night, they were short one PA The other one was stuck in an airport with a delayed flight. He was already two hours late due to high static electricity in the air which had grounded all flights in and out of New York, and he didn't know when he'd get there. Liselle Grady went to work to recruit a backup.

Dr. Debra Yeager was the attending physician, and Evan Presley was the senior resident. Fortunately, Dr. Presley was one of those doctors who liked to sew, because no one else on that shift would have chosen to spend the night in the suture room. Summer was when people stepped on things in their bare feet, used dull tools in their gardens, and played with fireworks. The waiting room was backed up with wounds. It had also been overflowing with heat related illness as one of the hottest summers in history was baking half of the planet.

Some patients were literally cooked. Brody Jones had signed two heat stroke patients over to Dewy. One was a sixty-two-year-old fisherman whose outboard engine died in the middle of the lake. By the time he was rescued by another boater, he had been drinking beer in the hot sun for more than three hours. Beer was the only beverage he'd brought with him. His little boat was reported to have a broken oarlock, a missing oar and no life preserver, in addition to a rusty old motor, and he hadn't been wearing a hat.

Upon admission, his temperature was one hundred six and he was semi-conscious. He had since lapsed into unconsciousness. When his wife was contacted, she swore she might kill him if he survived. She was furious that he'd been so stubbornly negligent about his own safety, but she made her way to the ER to support him.

He was cooled down with an ice bath, but the neurology resident expected his brain to continue to swell for another day or two, in which case they might have to drill some holes in his skull to ease the pressure on the brain and prevent further damage. He'd soon be on his way to the neurology ICU. His wife became hysterical when the neurologist explained that the man could wind up seriously disabled, and she signed herself into the ER for anxiety and depression. Brody referred her case to the psych resident.

A twenty-year-old woman who had recently started working nights in a factory had fallen asleep in a lounge chair on the south-facing terrace of her apartment, wearing just a halter-top and shorts. Her body clock and her job hadn't synched very well, and according to her roommate, she'd been using sleeping pills to get some daytime sleep.

When the roommate found her at four p.m. and tried to wake her up, she was as red as a beet and incoherent. Most of her front side was blistered and her eyes were swollen shut. More ominously, heat stroke had shut down her kidneys. She was about to be transferred to the ICU to start dialysis, but they were still waiting for a bed.

There were three more heat-whipped Sunday athletes who had managed to get out of the sun before their heat exhaustion turned into heat stroke. One had fainted, one had dizziness with vomiting, and one had a headache and was confused. They were all expected to fully recover with IV hydration.

That hot Sunday afternoon, some other severely sunburned patients had shown up, all teenaged girls. They mistakenly believed that if they put sunscreen on, it was okay to fry themselves at the poolside all day, instead of covering up or seeking shade when the sun was strongest. All the ER could do for most of them was advise cool showers and some anti-inflammatory treatment like aspirin or ibuprofen.

Brody also signed over the case of a teenager with a rattlesnake bite. His brother took a picture of the snake and compared to pictures on the Internet, it definitely looked like a rattler. They had been hiking when the snake popped out from under a rock and bit him on his sockless ankle. It struck again when they failed to get away from the snake because they wanted to take its picture. Anti-venom was just starting to alleviate his blurred vision and the numbness he felt all over, but he was still foaming at the mouth and having abdominal pain and labored breathing. Without the anti-venom, he probably would have died within a day.

A four-year-old girl presented with hundreds of porcupine quills in her hand. She had tried to pet what she thought was a 'pretty kitty' in her back yard. The PA had to keep her sedated for hours to get the quills out, but he worried that some of the quills had migrated into the flexor tendons. Ultrasound proved him right, and the little girl was waiting for a hand surgeon to take her to the OR for deep dissection and extraction.

Dewy saw a teenaged couple that had made love in a field. The girl's entire backside was a giant itchy rash, while her partner had managed to get the poison ivy resin on his genitals. While its contents were busy elsewhere, the guy's inside out underpants had been resting on top of the oily plant. The miserable couple got put on steroids and told to sit in oatmeal baths.

There was also the usual procession of babies, children and adults with earaches, sore throats, wheezing and chest pain, and then, things got a little too interesting. Liselle handed Dewy the chart of a five-year-old girl with bloody diarrhea. She looked really ill and her blood pressure was sky high. She was pale and puffy, and she had bruises all over. The family doctor had done stool cultures on Friday, but the results remained unknown. She was on an antibiotic but getting worse. Her labs showed severe anemia and kidney failure.

Dewy didn't know what was going on. When she asked Dr. Yeager for a consult, the seasoned physician immediately recognized what failing kidneys, bloody diarrhea and severe anemia were indicative of. Dewy and the little girl's family were informed about HUS, hemolytic-uremic syndrome.

A bacterium that went by the name of *E. coli 0157:H7*, releases a toxin that destroys red blood cells. The dead cells clog up the gut, the kidneys and other body systems. Without intensive supportive care, it was a fatal disease. There was no cure, but most children would recover if they underwent dialysis until their kidneys started to function again. Dr. Yeager called the pediatric nephrologist, and it was arranged for the little girl to be ambulanced to the ICU in the new children's hospital where the specialist could manage her case.

"Uh oh," Dr. Austin Smith said when he heard her story. "Another HUS kid was transferred here yesterday from the Pine Meadow ER. That four-year-old boy ate all kinds of stuff at a picnic sponsored by his preschool. Now he's in our ICU on dialysis and having seizures. What will the source be this time: lettuce, spinach, undercooked hamburgers, or maybe unpasteurized milk? Go ask your family if they went to a picnic a week ago Friday."

"Yes, they did," Dr. Yeager learned. "The youngest ones were also swimming in some kind of a kiddy pool, or should I say, they were wading and splashing in a cesspool. The family here estimates that there were more than a hundred people at the picnic, maybe a lot more. At least half of them were young children."

Dr. Austin called Dr. Debra back. "I talked to the nephrologist at University Hospital and they also have a case, a three-year-old who got admitted three days ago and is starting to recover. This looks like an outbreak, so I'm going to call the public health emergency hotline. This illness needs to get diagnosed before the victims go into kidney failure, and doctors need to know to avoid antibiotics, which can worsen HUS."

The story came out on the ten o'clock news and until about three a.m., CityStar ER was inundated with people who had attended the picnic, or who had been hanging out with someone who attended the picnic, erroneously believing that the infection might be contagious. Most had no symptoms and were told that HUS rarely affected healthy adults, even if they ate the contaminated food. Young children and people with immune disorders were the only ones considered vulnerable.

Many wanted to be tested anyway and those who had risk factors were signed in and screened for protein in their urine, an early sign. The urine dipstick enabled the PA to identify a case in a four-year-old boy. The child had attended the picnic but hadn't been in the pool because he had stitches in his knee. He was immediately transferred to the children's hospital for management by the specialist.

Dr. Yeager let the health department know that it probably wasn't the kiddy pool that harbored the infecting bacteria, but something they ate. Dr. Austin Smith called his counterpart in a neighboring state and found out that they had a few cases that weren't at the preschool picnic. If it turned out to be the same strain of E. coli, the source might more easily be traced.

Dewy and Brody were supposed to meet in an outdoor cafe for breakfast after she showered away the essence of ER. However, with the new knowledge of a multistate outbreak of a deadly disease from a yet to be identified food source, Dewy wondered if there was a safe place to eat. They wouldn't learn until a week later that the source of this HUS outbreak was unpasteurized apple juice.

Chapter Twenty-Nine

"Then let's have breakfast at my place," Brody said, "The sun doesn't hit the balcony until afternoon, so it should be pleasant. I've got eggs and stuff. We can have a champagne breakfast and then you can go home and sleep off your shift."

"What are you going to do on your day off?" Dewy asked.

"I was going to take a hike in Pine Canyon Park to look for some interesting stones to carve, but it's probably going to be too hot for that. Instead, I'm going to study for a few hours, hit the gym, and then I want to go see a new exhibit at the downtown art emporium. It's an international collection of political cartoons about climate change. I want to see how the rest of the world is illustrating their disgust with climate change denial."

Brody seemed very serious about climate change and about the 'stuff' he had to go with the eggs. Dewy watched him skillfully chop up an onion and a pepper in a few seconds with an incredibly deft hand, and cook it all up in a great big, fluffy cheese omelet, while he sautéed Canadian bacon. He served it with toast, orange juice spiked with champagne, and an impish smile on his boyish face. He knew he had impressed her. Dewy avoided the great smelling coffee he brewed in his built-in espresso machine. She'd be back on duty in ten hours and she hoped to get some daytime sleep.

As she watched Brody prepare their meal like a skilled chef, she felt embarrassed. Had he come to her dark little studio apartment, all she could have offered was instant coffee and cinnamon toast, and she could barely do that without burning the toast. She wasn't into shopping or cooking. Her typical breakfast was junk from a vending machine, if she did notice that she was hungry. After a nightshift, she was often too tired to eat, but Brody's companionship seemed to be a good antidote for her fatigue, as well as an appetite stimulant.

"Is this your typical breakfast?" she asked. Brody's culinary talent not only intimidated her, but Dewy was amazed that he had all of these ingredients on hand.

"I'm really big on protein for breakfast. My brain needs the protein, or I can't think straight. I'm not at all adverse to eating a steak or hamburger for breakfast, or left-over Chinese food, if that's what's in the fridge."

Dewy almost gagged at the thought of steak for breakfast, and she decided that hamburger-eating Brody wasn't all that environmentally conscience. She was a junk food vegetarian herself, but not a purist, so she took a few bites of the bacon to be polite. "Then, I'll bet you work out, don't you?"

"This building has a fantastic gym, and I do manage to get there a few times a week. There's a gym in the hospital housing, isn't there?"

Dewy wasn't about to admit that she had only seen that gym once, on the day that she was shown around the building and given her apartment key. "It's a pretty nice gym, but we spend so much time indoors, that when I do have the time and energy to exercise, I like to walk outdoors. Of course, it's been too hot outdoors, so I haven't done much of that lately. I really should try to get to the gym more often," she lied.

Dewy hated the gym and smelling other people's perspiration. She liked to skate, ski, hike, cycle and swim, or anything else that felt like she was floating through space. The gym stifled the sense of freedom that she found so appealing when she was gliding down a mountain or cruising on her bike.

She thought of treadmills and weights as the antitheses of natural motion, and she didn't get yoga at all. Yoga was just one more way for people to spend more time sitting; though now they were sitting on a mat on the floor, instead of in a chair all day at work, and on the couch all evening watching TV, or in their car going to and from wherever else they were going to sit.

One of the interesting things about working in the ER was that there was almost never an opportunity to sit, unless you were repairing a laceration. Even the computer stations were more conducive to standing than sitting. She suddenly became concerned that psychiatrists probably spent their whole day sitting.

"Do you do any sports?" she asked Brody.

"I played soccer in high school, but I quit after my father saw an article in a medical journal about soccer players winding up brain-damaged from heading the ball. I also used to play competitive tennis, but then I wound up with tendonitis in my wrist and ruining my hands just doesn't fit in with my career plans, so I only play recreationally these days, or did before med school took over my life.

"I do love to ski. Before my father left us, our family would go on ski vacations to Banff or Colorado over Christmas, and we'd ski in California on winter weekends. Up until med school, my dad and I would go on a boys-only ski vacation once a year, so I've skied in Switzerland, France and Austria, but I have no time for that now. I'll be thrilled if I get to ski even once this year. Sometimes, I fantasize about having a surgical practice in a ski town, like Aspen or Tahoe."

Dewy had a similar fantasy. In her dreams, she had a multilingual psychiatry practice in Chamonix, France or Zermatt, Switzerland.

The newest feature of the dream was having a big dog like Kemosabe sitting in her office, giving love to the people who needed love, and warning her about the people she shouldn't trust. She'd also have to learn Italian if she settled in Zermatt. In that little town they spoke French, German, and Italian.

"I love those mountain resort towns. They are so quaint, yet sophisticated. Daddy Dave was on a gold mine project in Slovakia when I was a junior in college, so I took a year off from school and my sister Daisy and I ski bummed our way around Europe. It was the best year of my life, but you know what was so amazing? We weren't special for speaking so many languages. Many Europeans speak multiple languages, and almost everyone can speak English. It makes the U.S. look so, so narrow-minded, so *eng-stir-nig*, my father would say in German.

"My stepdad is now stationed in Norway for a gold mine renovation, and I'm going to go visit on my vacation in January. There are over a hundred ski resorts there, and I've read that the snow is abundant, and the slopes are practically empty. My sister Daisy and her husband are going to come too. It may be the only time I'll get to see my family this year. My little sister Dahlia won't be able to join us because of her school schedule, but she's coming to visit me at the end of August."

"Norway sound's fantastic. Lucky you. My dad goes all over Europe to ski, but I don't believe he's ever skied in Scandinavia. I'll have to tell him about Norway.

"So, I want to hear about your last night's shift," Brody said. "How'd all the heat exhaustion people do? I've yet to have a shift where I don't see something I know nothing about, and yesterday it was *crypto-spor-idium*. I saw a family with two little kids with fever, vomiting and watery diarrhea for a week. The little one was seriously dehydrated.

"I mentioned this family to Dr. Stone, and she said she'd seen some kids the day before with similar symptoms, and when she heard about this family, she said a week was kind of too long for most stomach viruses. We were discussing these cases with Dr. Schwartz at the triage desk, when Xray said he knew of another case that Dr. Volkov had seen. That set off an alarm for Dr. Schwartz and he called the other families, and then we realized that all of these little kids were going to the same daycare and the facility has a wading pool.

"Cryptosporidium is a parasite that gets passed from animal or human feces into water. People are supposed to wait two weeks after having a diarrheal illness before they swim in a public pool, but in the hot weather, nobody follows that rule.

"Also, the daycare center allowed kids in diapers to use the pool. They thought rubber pants over the diapers would be protective, but that assumes that these tots wont tug at the elastic around their legs, letting some water in and out. Any child who gets contaminated water in their nose or mouth could ingest the parasite's eggs. Then, depending on the size of the ingestion and the host's vulnerability, symptoms might show up in a few days or a few weeks. Dr. Schwartz said the health department will likely close the pool for the season because it's so hard to kill crypto."

"Do anti-parasite drugs kill crypto?" Dewy asked.

Brody shook his head. "There's just one drug that helps with the diarrhea and weight loss, but it can cost about a thousand dollars per person. The family we saw on Sunday had to wait for a pharmacist to get preapproval from some unresponsive paper pusher working for a stingy insurer before he could dispense it.

"The other family that Dr. Stone saw was uninsured and for them, access to the drug seemed hopeless. American health care kind of looks like a caste system. People of means can access treatment, but we have to tell the poor people that they'll just have to suffer. What kind of a country does that to its citizens, especially little kids?"

"It's ludicrous," Dewy agreed. She gave Brody the follow-up on the patients he had signed over to her, and then, told him about the child with HUS. "Wow, is that a wicked infection! I'd heard about these E. coli outbreaks in the news, but I didn't realize how awful this illness is until I saw it up close and personal. That little girl looked like she was on death's doorstep. It's terrifying to think that there are other little kids with HUS out there who won't get diagnosed in time. They'll wind up dead or on dialysis for as long as they live."

Brody looked troubled. "You know, I saw a little kid yesterday with fever and bloody diarrhea for maybe just two days, but he looked kind of sick, and now that I think about it, he was too pale. I wonder if he could have HUS." Brody immediately called the ER and asked Gus to follow up with that family and have the child rechecked.

"I had another interesting experience yesterday," Brody said. "A sixty-year-old real estate agent named Vicki presented for cough and fever. A chest x-ray showed pneumonia. I was going to discharge her on oral antibiotics, but Vicki asked me to contact her primary care doctor because she had previously had a bad pneumonia that put her in the hospital. She was worried about being on the right drug.

"Amazingly, I was able to get a hold of her internist, Dr. Hughs, and he was pushing for admission. He told me that Vicki was unaware that a radiologist had been worried about scarring of her lungs during her prior bout of pneumonia. When Vicki was asked about asbestos exposure, she revealed that as a child, it was her chore to meet her father at the doorway when he came home from his construction job and put his work clothes in the washing machine. Dr. Hughs had chosen not to tell Vicki about the possibility of asbestosis, a fatal disease, because they weren't sure, and he didn't want to unnecessarily worry her. Now he was very worried about her and he wanted her admitted.

"So, not knowing what to do, I consulted Dr. Presley. He didn't think Vicki's oxygen level justified admission, and he recommended discharging her on a strong oral antibiotic.

"Just then, the internal medicine chief resident was in the ER because he was admitting another patient, so I asked him about Vicki's case. He advised an antibiotic shot to start, followed by oral antibiotics at home.

"So now, I had three differing opinions and I sought a consult with Dr. Schwartz. He listened to Vicki's lungs for a rather long time, and then he had a respiratory therapist check her breathing capacity, which was quite abnormal in spite of her good oxygen level. Dr. Ted concluded that Vicki's lung function was maybe too compromised for the degree of pneumonia we saw on the chest film. He recommended we start intravenous antibiotics and observe her in the ER for another twelve hours. I went with Dr. Ted's plan.

"Later, I got to talk with our amazing ER director, and I told him it was disconcerting to have gotten four different opinions about management of Vicki's case. I don't think I'll ever forget what he said to me. Dr. Ted said: 'Are you feeling confused about how to appropriately diagnose and treat your patients? Are you perplexed by all of the cases that don't fit the textbook pattern? Does it seem like what you learned last year doesn't apply to this year, or that what seemed like a good plan for patient A won't work for patient B? Are you befuddled by the contrary opinions given by different expert consultants? Do you feel like there's always a variety of answers to your questions, but never one correct answer?'

"I said yes, that's exactly how I've been feeling since I started my internship."

Dewy said, "Me too."

"Dr. Schwartz said, 'Good! Then you are learning medicine.'"

"Well, thanks for that tidbit. That will take some digestion, and so will this fantastic breakfast. Thanks so much, Brody. Enjoy your day off while I go get some sleep."

Chapter Thirty

efore getting into bed, Dewy checked her E-mail, and there it was: the message from Alex that she had been both anticipating and dreading.

To My Dearest Dewy,

It is with great sorrow that I must tell you that things have drastically changed for me in the past few months. Instead of starting my residency as planned, I enrolled in a program for gender reassignment.

I think I've known on some level, maybe since kindergarten, that I was never meant to be a man, but I didn't let that knowledge rule my consciousness until very recently. Whenever those feelings would surface, I would deny and bury them.

It was during my elective rotation in an oncologist's office in our last semester of med school that I finally woke up to the conflict that has burned deep in my subconscious for so long. I was examining a fifty-six-year-old high school principal who had just finished radiation treatment for prostate cancer, when the man broke down and started crying that he had finally recognized that he was supposed to be a woman. However, now that he had finally admitted it to himself, and now that sex-change surgery was becoming somewhat normal; he felt like he was too old, too unhealthy, and too rooted in his community to make the change. He cried because he felt like his whole life had been a sham and would continue to be so, and for reasons he couldn't explain, I was the first person he had ever told.

I believe the reason that this man decided to share his secret with me, is because he saw his own reflection in me, and then, I saw myself in that poor soul as though he were a mirror. I don't want to reach his stage of life and regret that my whole life has been a sham.

I am now undergoing counseling and hormone therapy. In a few months I will be seeing a plastic surgeon to start the processes of getting rid of my beard, feminizing my face, and doing top surgery. I haven't yet decided about bottom surgery.

I hope to start my residency next July as a woman, and my residency advisor has been very supportive. In as much as taking this first step was so difficult, I now understand that the whole lengthy process is difficult. I've been counseled that it takes most men two years to fully transition, and three to five years is not unusual. Yet, now that I have taken the first step, I know that this is what I must do. I have never been more certain of anything in my life.

I will always love you Dewy, but I presently don't know what my future will be, and I don't want you to wait for me while I figure things out. I pray that you can forgive me for what might seem like deception, but hope you know I did not deliberately deceive you. I was honestly attracted to you, I still love you, and I hope you will continue to be my friend.

Always,

Alex

With tears drenching her keyboard, Dewy read Alex's words five, maybe six times. Her first feeling was numbness. It all seemed unreal. Then she felt overwhelmingly sad for Alex and for how painful their relationship must have been for him. Then she felt sad for herself. She had not only invested three years in the relationship, but also her heart. She felt like her heart had been breaking ever since she and Alex had gone their separate ways. Now her heart felt like it was completely fractured. It was actually hurting.

Then she felt anger, not at poor Alex, but at herself. How could she have not known? Or did she know and like Alex, was in denial? Weren't there obvious clues like his gentleness and his empathetic nature? She had thought he could be soft like that because he was comfortable with his masculinity. Wow, had she misread the man!

For a few minutes she wondered if she might be gay. Was her attraction to Alex really attraction to another woman? If Alex completed his transition and then wanted to be with her instead of a man, would she still want to be with him? Her? If she really loved Alex, did it matter whether Alex was a man or a woman? She didn't know the answer to that question, which made her feel helpless and stupid.

She took some solace in the fact that she was maybe starting to feel a little bit of an attraction to Brody, baby face and all. But Brody had a feminine side too, so she wasn't sure what sparked the attraction, and she felt utterly confused, *danxin* again, she thought in Mandarin. If she couldn't figure out what the importance of gender was with regard to a loving relationship, how could she possibly help anyone else struggling with that conflict?

Then she got really disgusted with herself. How could she be a psychiatrist helping other people to sort out relationships, when for three years she had been in a relationship that she obviously didn't understand, with a person she didn't really know? How could she think she had the capacity to see other people's issues, when she was apparently so oblivious to the tormenting issue that Alex must have struggled with for their whole time together? Dr. Dewy Meadows, who thought her talent in life was psychoanalyzing people, was just as clueless as everyone else. Maybe she was living a lie too.

There was no way she could sleep. She wished there was someone she could talk to, but the only person who had truly been her confidant throughout medical school was Alex. Their relationship had been so exclusive that she hadn't really bonded with anyone else.

Dewy had peripheral friends from college, but no one with whom she had maintained a close relationship. Her childhood hadn't afforded her the opportunity to cement friendships. Between second grade and college, her stepfather's roving assignments had caused them to move five times, always leaving friends behind. Perhaps, books had been her best friends.

Feeling devastated and lonely, she soothed herself by reading. She read about gender dysphoria and gender reassignment procedures, and her sympathy for Alex immeasurably increased. She came to appreciate how desperately unhappy he must have been to be willing to go this route.

After a few hours of beating up on herself, she did the one thing she realized she needed to do to make her brain stop quaking. She composed a dozen drafts that she erased. Finally, she wrote:

Dearest Alex,

It must have been so hard for you to make this decision and let me know, but I'm very grateful that you cared enough to tell me. I could not have imagined that this was the issue that was driving us apart, but now I understand.

Please know that no matter what, I will always be your friend, and I can't wait to meet the new you, when you are ready.

Love always,

Dewy

She clicked the send button, wondering if she would ever even hear from Alex again. She suspected he would want to close the door on his old life after he, she, carved out a new one for herself.

Dewy spent some time erasing pictures from her phone, though she kept a few photos that reminded her of how happy they had once been.

Finally, she cried herself to sleep.

Chapter Thirty-One

D r. Brody Jones was alarmed by Dewy's appearance when she signed over the patients from her nightshift. Her eyes were red rimmed, and she looked more tired and distressed than he had previously seen her. Her fire engine red scrubs just seemed to amplify her hospital pallor and the dark circles under her puffy eyes. As they rounded between rooms, Brody came to appreciate that Dewy had experienced one more catastrophic shift.

The 'black cloud' comment that Dr. Schwartz had made, had become another topic of gossip amongst the ER staff, and now, to her repertoire of attracting patients injured in bus crashes, fires, and mass shootings and poisonings, they would add the hazmat incident.

CityStar ER took care of more than half of the twenty-some people who were exposed to chlorine gas. Some were taken to other ERs. The victims were all male laborers from a factory that produced PVC pipe, plastic tubing made out of polyvinyl chloride.

A tank of chlorine gas had been delivered to the factory at about five p.m. A few hours later, some of the nightshift workers noticed burning of their eyes and noses. Shortly thereafter, most were complaining of shortness of breath and chest pain.

A foreman went to investigate. He could smell the chlorine gas as soon as he opened the door to the storage room where the tank had been deposited. The tank gauge showed a slight drop in pressure, indicating a slow leak. He pushed a lever that immediately closed off all the air ducts in the storage room, but he was in too much respiratory distress to be able to even try to put on a gas mask and do anything to stop the leak. He escaped to a loading dock, called for help, and started evacuating the workers. He was well aware that exposure to chlorine gas could be rapidly fatal.

"There's no antidote for chlorine poisoning," Dewy said. "All we can do for these poor victims is give comfort care. They're all on humidified oxygen and breathing treatments. We had to recruit respiratory therapists from all over the hospital, and we had to round-up extra nurses to help get their eyes flushed out. Some of the men with thick dry hair smelled of chlorine gas, because their hair must have absorbed it. They got showered and shampooed.

"We've got them all in hospital gowns and their clothes are being aired out on the hospital roof. Someone from the company just delivered some t-shirts and shorts, so when we discharge these men, we don't have to send them off with their butts hanging out of their stupid hospital gowns. If they want to keep their contaminated clothing, the clothes should be double bagged until they can be washed.

"We discharged about half of them who improved with breathing treatments, but we have five here who are still coughing and wheezing. The older workers and the smokers seem to have been most severely affected. We admitted one elderly smoker whose lactic acid level was in the danger zone, and we had to admit the foreman who saved everyone else, because his heart rhythm went bonkers. They've all had baseline chest films and EKGs, because some of them could go on to have chronic breathing problems or heart arrhythmias after this exposure.

"Dr. Patel says that those who can keep their oxygen levels up for an hour after they've been taken off supplemental oxygen can be discharged. They'll all need follow-ups in the pulmonary and cardiology clinics.

"In room seven we've got two overdoses, a sixteen-year-old who maybe tried to drink herself to death, and an elderly woman who maybe took too many of her diabetes pills. The alcohol case got her stomach pumped and her alcohol level has started to come down. She needs to be cleared by psych and a social worker before discharge. Her family in the waiting area is rowdy and rude and they all smell like they've been drinking.

"The older woman was brought in by her son at about four this morning. She was in distress and her blood pressure and blood sugar were really low. The son brought her meds in and her blood level of metformin was double the upper limits of safe. I had no idea that metformin can be seriously lethal, but apparently the death rate from an overdose can be as high as eighty percent. The son said his mother has started to show signs of dementia and he thinks she got confused and took too many doses.

"She's on her way to dialysis as soon as they finish their shift change, but now there's a kink in the story. A little while ago, Nurse Hana overheard the son talking on his phone, and she became suspicious that it was maybe the son who overdosed his mother.

"The man has been acting like a very devoted child, but maybe a little too devoted. Hana heard him discussing who's going to get what when she dies. It could all be very innocent, but we're taking Hana's suspicion seriously. There's a plain-clothes detective in the waiting area. He'll intercept the son as soon as they come to transfer his mother. To be honest, the son gave me the creeps.

"I've got one more to sign over to you, though he will be going to the OR pretty soon. He's an adolescent rape victim who also incurred blunt head trauma. He was found in a parking lot in a pool of blood, conscious but incoherent. The police are still trying to identify him, and the colorectal surgeon is on his way. He's sedated now."

"Are you okay. Dewy?" Brody asked. "You look like this shift beat you up pretty badly."

"Bad, bad shift, Brody. I don't think I was cut out for the horrors of emergency medicine, but I'm determined to get through this rotation, black cloud and all. I just need to get some sleep and to put this night behind me."

Chapter Thirty-Two

It was a sumptuous, sunny summer day, eighty degrees with a gentle sweet breeze. It was the first time that Dewy and Brody had shared a day off without one of them being post-duty. They decided to take advantage of the pleasant weather and the fact that neither one of them was exhausted. They rented bicycles and toured around the city, noticing things one never sees when whizzing by in a cab or bus. They stopped for lunch in the exquisite garden of a small Persian café.

"So how was your dayshift yesterday?" Dewy asked, not wanting to talk about anything personal. She had never told Brody about Alex and she saw no point in now telling him that her most precious relationship had just gone the way of a cassette tape.

"Are we really going to talk shop?' Brody asked.

"Not much else going on in my life," Dewy made an effort to smile. "Anything exciting happening in your off-duty hours?"

"Well now that you mention it, not much. It does feel like we eat, sleep, and breathe medicine. Every single shift introduces me to something I'm ignorant of, and I go from the ER to the computer to read, read, read.

"Do you know what you get if every single day, all day long, you read medical journals? You just get behind. It's impossible to keep up with all of the new information that keeps getting churned out almost daily, let alone learn the basics.

"When my dad gave me his library of surgical textbooks, he said that surgery's the one specialty that doesn't change that much, so the books still have value. He threw out all of his medical texts. He said that after three decades, they were almost completely obsolete."

"I really don't know how ER docs and primary care providers can possibly keep up with all of the new developments in *every* field." Dewy added. "I try to read a few psychiatry articles every day, and I can't even process all of that information. How can anyone keep up with all the new stuff in cardiology, pediatrics, pharmacology, and all of the other specialties? I don't know how a specialist can even keep up with all of the new information in just their *own* field."

"My mom Josie has a great saying about specialization. Actually, it's a quote from a famous writer, Robert A. Heinlein, the reputed 'Dean of Science Fiction.' Whenever Mom would change from one art medium to another, which was often, she would recite this quote." Brody Googled the famous words:

> A human being should be able to change a diaper, plan an invasion, butcher a hog, conn (steer) a ship, design a building, write a sonnet, balance accounts, build a wall, set a bone, comfort the dying, take orders, give orders, cooperate, act alone, solve equations, analyze a new problem, pitch manure, program a computer, cook a tasty meal, fight efficiently, die gallantly. Specialization is for insects.

"I do love science fiction," Dewy said, "and I think I read some of Heinlein's novels when I was a kid. I read all of the sci-fi books I could find in my school libraries, but after a while, that stuff sort of mishmashes into a giant jumble of genius and insanity. In high school, I switched my reading genre to psychologic thrillers. I still love to read those.

"If Robert A. Heinlein is right, then I must be an insect, perhaps a dung beetle, cause I sure no how to step in it. I'm going to have my sister Dahlia make a new set of scrubs for me, sky blue with black cloud silhouettes. Maybe I'll have her embroider *nuage noir* on the pocket; that's 'black cloud' in French; in Mandarin, its *wuyun*. For me, ER medicine is a nasty storm, a genuine horror show. Since I started this rotation, I've seen way too much human cruelty, including other rape cases, but that brutal case I signed over to you the other morning, the teenaged boy; that one gave me nightmares."

"I get that Dewy, but when I see this stuff, I remind myself that it's simply a fact of life, that some humans are genetically and/or environmentally programmed to hurt others. We are a flawed species. Seeing these cases is the training that will make you a more perceptive psychiatrist. I had a case yesterday that will certainly make me a more perceptive physician.

"The patient was a forty-two-year-old nurse who works in a rehab facility and lives alone. At seven in the morning, she called her sister and said that when she woke up, her left breast was twice the size of the right. Her sister brought her in, and I could not believe the enormous degree of swelling that supposedly just happened overnight, out of the blue.

"Anyway, I tried to get a history and Stella, the patient, wasn't quite making sense. To be blunt, she sounded totally loony. I took her sister aside and she told me that Stella hadn't been herself for a few weeks. She was becoming increasingly irritable, forgetful, and unreasonable.

"So, I'm assuming she has dementia, and she must have somehow traumatized the breast and she's cognitively so out if it, that she doesn't know how she did it, or doesn't remember it happened. But then, I thought she's really too young to be that demented, so I consulted Dr. Volkov. It took her a second to make the diagnosis.

"Apparently, inflammatory breast cancer is a rare and very aggressive type of cancer. Rapidly growing tumor cells block the flow of lymph in the tissue, and a fluid backup can very suddenly expand the whole breast. Dr. Olga said that Stella's confusion and reported behavior changes were probably due to brain metastasis. MRI proved her right.

"So here I'm thinking this poor woman's cognitive problem caused her to have a breast problem, when it was the breast problem that caused the brain problem. I'm so glad I didn't just send her home with ice packs.

"Dr. Olga's lesson to me for the day was: 'Always assume they're sick before you assume that they're crazy.' We sometimes think normal people just snap, but if you look carefully enough, you might find a biologic reason for why they've lost their mind. But speaking of crazy, let me tell you about the next chapter in the lives of the infamous Farrells."

"Oh no! Which kid this time?" The mixture of surprise and pouting on Dewy's face would have been worth a photo. It was how Brody would sculpt her if he were going to do a remodel.

"So, Carol must like you better," Dewy scoffed. "I'm really sorry I dragged you into that abyss, but it's nice to know that you're a genuine snake charmer. So, which of her poor kids was she there for this time?"

"It wasn't for any of the kids. She came in because the housekeeper tripped over a cat and went down, hitting her hand on a coffee table. She fractured the metacarpals of her pinky and ring finger. Nice lady, Tia Williams, but so weather-beaten, she looks much older than she actually is. Ortho will pin the fractures when the swelling goes down, and Carol was very concerned about Tia's ability to work.

I got the impression that while Carol runs to doctors, Tia runs that household."

"I've wondered how Carol manages it all," Dewy said.

"Carol also gave me an update on the kids. Gerald has turned the corner with his cat scratch disease, and Merrill is getting his smile back, but Darryl is still screaming.

"The baby had a high manganese level and so did Carol. She went to see a toxicologist at the State Health Department. They didn't recommend chelation, just avoidance of the contaminated water. The toxicologist suggested getting the baby checked for kidney stones, so they did that at University Hospital; no stones, but more sedation and radiation. Carol is still raging that all of the damn doctors still don't have any answers while Darryl is going to start to glow in the dark.

"Then she gave me the lowdown on Bojo. He's old and deaf and sometimes he fails to get out of people's way. It's a major cat disability Carol said. She couldn't stay and elaborate because she was on her way to the vet. She thought Bojo might have incurred some broken ribs when Tia tripped over him. He meowed when she tried to pick him up. Only a cat person such as myself would understand. Meow."

Dewy laughed. She couldn't remember the last time she had laughed. Is that how doctors survived, she wondered, by laughing at the crazy people they took care of all day?

Laughter had been missing in her life. She and Alex got through med school by renting comical movies and laughing themselves stupid. Then she thought about the crazy people, specifically Carol Farrell and poor screaming Darryl, and now, a hurt housekeeper and an injured cat. Nothing to laugh at there!

"How can the baby's problem just be colic if it doesn't end, *Monsieur* Cat Daddy? There are a lot of theories about colic, but Dr. Olga's favorite is that colicky infants grow up to be perfectionistic adults. Their colic goes away once they start to be able to do things for themselves, like sit up and hold a bottle. The crying is just their way of saying they don't like being helpless infants, dependent on others for every little thing."

Brody's eyebrows arched. "Actually, the baby was sitting up and holding her own bottle, now that you mention it. She wasn't eating though. I think she was just teething on the nipple. She's always sitting facing away from Carol and she never smiles. I've seen enough babies over the past few weeks to know that little Darryl looks much too serious. Something psychologic is going on there," Brody speculated.

"Always assume they're sick before you assume they're crazy." Dewy reminded him.

Chapter Thirty-Three

"I've got Carol Farrell out in the waiting room with the scream-ing baby," Nina the admitting clerk warned. "Do you want me to bring them back?"

Triage nurse Liselle sent Nurse Gus to the waiting room to get them, and she informed Doctors Ted Schwartz and Dewy Meadows that the Farrells were back again. It was six-thirty on a Thursday morning and the ER was almost empty. Dr. Schwartz was finish-ing up with an asthma patient, and Dr. Meadows was monitoring a pregnant woman in premature labor who was waiting for a bed in the obstetric unit.

"Darryl will not stop screaming," Carol said. "It started an hour ago and she just won't stop. Someone has to do something. This has become unbearable and I'm afraid I'm going to lose it if we can't get some help. I'm at the end of my rope with this screaming."

Gus hooked Darryl up to a brand-new pediatric monitor. Dr. Ted followed Dewy into the room to see the infant he had heard so much about. Although he was obviously familiar with Carol, she wasn't at all cordial to him. Uncharacteristically, her hair was uncombed, she seemed jittery, and she appeared to have a fresh coffee stain down the front of her crisp white blouse.

"Is this very different from her usual pattern of screaming?" Dewy asked, just as Darryl finally stopped. The baby girl was sweat-ing, and her face was wet with tears.

"Well, I've been taking her to a pediatric acupuncturist, and I thought she was doing a little better. Her screaming fits seemed less intense and for shorter time periods, starting after her second treatment. She's had three treatments so far."

"What does the acupuncturist do?' Dewy asked.

"She's an elderly Chinese lady. She barely speaks English, and she's hard to understand. A Chinese dentist that uses Harold's lab recommended her. He told us that not only is she trained in classical Chinese acupuncture, but she also does Japanese scalp acupuncture and Korean hand acupuncture, whatever any of that is. He also said that she's a medical intuitive, an unusually gifted diagnostician. She's only really known in the Asian community.

"When we're there, she spends a lot of time feeling Darryl's pulses, and looking at her tongue. She's a really small person with very small hands. She uses a soft brush and a little metal ball on a stick to rub up and down and press in places on Darryl's limbs, torso and scalp. Then, she puts tiny seeds on the back of Darryl's pinkies and anchors them with ribbons, and I'm supposed to keep them there until the next bath. She also burns stinky stuff called moxa in an incense burner. She says quality moxa for babies is very expensive, and that's why she charges so much. It smells like marijuana to me, but Darryl seems really relaxed when we're in the office, which is more like a child's bedroom than an office.

"After the last two treatments, Darryl got through the rest of the day without a screaming fit. Her last treatment was Monday, and she seemed better on Tuesday and Wednesday, but this morning, she screamed as desperately as I've ever heard. This is not colic. Something terrible is hurting this baby and you doctors need to figure it out and do something about it. My whole family is going crazy with this." Carol's face was reddening.

"How can I get in touch with the acupuncturist?" Dewy asked.

"You speak Chinese? Unless she's talking price, I can't understand her."

"Actually, I speak Mandarin. How can I contact her?"

"I have her number in my phone. Here it is. She practices in her house, so maybe you can reach her now."

Dr. Ted examined Darryl while she was quiet, as Dewy made the call. Dewy's Mandarin was much better than the woman's English, and the acupuncturist was very glad she called because she thought the baby had a weak heart, *ruo de xinzang;* very weak, *feichang ruo.*

Dewy remembered seeing an EKG in Darryl's records from University Hospital from when they sedated her to examine her eyes. It was read as normal. She pulled it up from the computer and showed it to Dr. Ted, as she told him about the acupuncturist's opinion.

"I was just a little kid when my family lived in Korea, but our experience there gave us an appreciation for acupuncture. It cured my mom of migraine headaches and got rid of my sister's asthma. I actually once toyed with the idea of going to acupuncture school."

"I saw some amazing acupuncture results when I worked with international doctors during the Gulf War," Dr. Ted said. "It didn't work for all of our injured soldiers, but it helped many of them with pain, especially some that suffered from phantom limb pain."

Dr. Ted's eyes widened as he looked at the EKG from when Darryl was four months old. Maybe it wasn't as normal as had been determined at the time. As he measured the millimeters of the squiggly lines, it appeared that the electrical energy generated by the baby's heart was ever so slightly diminished, not enough for the study to have been called abnormal, but enough to jive with what this acupuncturist claimed.

He had Gus obtain a new EKG and the results were outright shocking. The study showed that Darryl had just had a major heart attack. Dr. Schwartz ordered a cardiac enzyme panel and a chest x-ray, and then he explained to Dewy, Carol and Gus, why poor little Darryl had been screaming since nine weeks of age.

"Mrs. Farrell, I regret to have to inform you that your daughter appears to have an extremely rare congenital heart defect. There is most likely an abnormality of the artery that provides most of the heart muscle with its blood supply. That artery is called the left coronary artery, the LCA for short. The LCA is supposed to come from the aorta at the top of the heart, but Darryl's LCA probably doesn't start where it's supposed to. Instead, it probably stems off of the pulmonary artery, the PA, lower down in the heart. I believe that Darryl may have something called ALCAPA syndrome, which is an abbreviation for Anomalous Left Coronary Artery coming off of the Pulmonary Artery. It's very rare.

"When the abnormal LCA doesn't deliver enough blood to the heart muscle, the muscle has a hard time contracting and pumping, and it gets tired and crampy. In other words, the muscle becomes ischemic and it hurts. It causes the nasty chest pain we call angina, or *angina pectoris*, pain of the chest. It's what we see in older people who have clogged coronary arteries.

"When the heart is so starved for blood that it can no longer adequately pump the blood to the rest of the body, that's called heart failure. A heart surgeon can try to open the arteries up with stents or perform open-heart surgery and replace the bad arteries with healthier blood vessels taken from another body part. That's what we call CABG or 'cabbage,' short for Coronary Artery Bypass Grafting.

"Darryl will need for her heart arteries to be restructured, and she may need to have blood vessels harvested from elsewhere in her body. How they fix the heart's circulation will depend on what can be seen on imaging. Newer imaging techniques can show how the blood flows within the heart's arteries without the invasiveness of catherization.

"The reason Darryl screams when she eats, is because for infants, sucking down a meal is hard work. The muscles of the tongue, throat and gut all need extra blood to do their jobs, just like your leg muscles need more blood if you start to run. So, sucking down a bottle means the heart must pump a little harder and faster, but then, the heart muscle doesn't get enough blood to do that; so, that's when Darryl gets chest pain. She cries until the pain stops, and then she's hungry enough to try to finish her meal. It takes even more work for an infant to get milk from the breast than from the bottle, which is why she probably had a hard time breast-feeding.

"It's also common for people with bad coronary arteries to get chest pain around six in the morning. That's when daytime hormones kick in and demand more work by the heart."

Carol unclenched her teeth. "So, if Darryl was born with this abnormal artery, why was she a quiet, peaceful little baby for her first two months of life?"

"Good question! I'll try to explain. In fetal life, and in the early life of a newborn, the heart circulation is still developing, and there's enough pressure in both the LCA and the PA for the heart muscle to get enough blood. However, around two months of age, as the baby is rapidly growing and becoming more physically active, there are pressure changes in the artery connections, and then in ALCAPA, the left coronary artery no longer gets its fair share of the blood supply. The heart will try to develop new blood vessels to compensate for the deprivation, but the collateral circulation can't always develop as fast as the baby grows. Infants typically double their weight in the first five months of life, so there's a whole lot of growing going on. If my diagnosis is correct, Darryl's problem is surgically fixable."

"Surgery is the only way to treat this?" Carol asked. She was almost shaking.

"There are medications that can ease her chest pain until we get her to surgery, and we will start those immediately; but without surgery, she has a very poor chance of survival.

"We need to transfer Darryl's care to the pediatric cardiology team at the new children's hospital. CityStar's pediatric heart surgeon is highly qualified and experienced. In the meantime, Darryl needs to be on a cardiac monitor and on medications that will reduce the work of the heart and help protect her from arrhythmias." Dr. Ted entered the medication orders into the computer as he spoke.

"Is this hereditary?" Carol asked, looking even more agitated.

"It's not. Nobody knows why this malformation of the heart's blood vessels just shows up in a tiny percent of people who are otherwise healthy."

"How come you know about this, and not one of the other doctors that Darryl has seen knew about it?" Carol asked. "We've been to more doctors than I can count."

"It's extremely unfortunate that ALCAPA tends to get written off as colic, Mrs. Farrell. ALCAPA is extremely rare, and most doctors have never heard of it, and they just don't expect healthy-looking little babies to be having heart attacks.

"There is nothing on a physical exam or on standard lab tests that would have shown that Darryl has ALCAPA. It usually only gets diagnosed when it's bad enough to be seen on an EKG. They did do an EKG on Darryl some weeks ago, which we have here in the records from University Hospital. However, at the time they did it,

Darryl's problem hadn't progressed enough to show up on an EKG, so they didn't have a reason to suspect it."

"But you suspected it," Carol argued. She seemed a little less flustered.

"Mrs. Farrell, I spent several decades of my career as a cardiovascular surgeon, and I never once saw a case of infantile ALCAPA. The only reason I've even heard of it is because there's a milder form of it that very rarely shows up in adults, and then only on a post-mortem exam when a healthy young person suddenly mysteriously dies.

"When a coroner looks at the heart of such a victim, they find that lots of collateral blood vessels developed in these people to supply the heart with the blood that the LCA wasn't providing. Then one day, the stress on the heart is too great, the collateral circulation can't meet the demand, and the heart gives out. I saw just one case once in my four decades as a doctor. It was the case of a young healthy soldier who unexpectedly died while doing physical training on a hot day. His EKG had been perfectly normal upon induction into the army.

"The good news, Mrs. Farrell, is that Darryl doesn't have to live with this pain anymore. Her problem is fixable. You were so smart to recognize that this wasn't just colic, because that's what ALCAPA usually gets called, and many cases only get diagnosed after the baby dies."

Darryl's cardiac enzymes came back elevated, and she was immediately ambulanced to the cardiac care unit at the children's hospital.

~~~

Dr. Brody Jones's next internship rotation just happened to be in surgery. By special request, he got to scrub in on Darryl Farrell's open-heart procedure.

He was mesmerized by the complex, delicate operation performed inside the baby's tiny chest cavity, and he was totally captivated by the manual finesse of the pediatric heart surgeon who performed the procedure and saved the baby's life.

~~~

On her next rotation in pediatrics, Dr. Dewy Meadows got to participate in Darryl Farrell's post-operative care.

Dewy just happened to be in the room on the second day after the surgery, when six-month-old Darryl smiled at her mother and her grandmother for the very first time in her life.

Chapter Thirty-Four

Dear Alexa,

I saw an article about your breakthrough cancer research, and I obtained your email address from a local oncologist who contributed to one of your papers. I would not have recognized you from the newspaper picture. You are quite the pretty woman.

If only your mother could know that you may be the physician who cures the cancer that took her away from you when you were seven years old. I sometimes thought that having lost a parent at age seven was part of what drew us together.

In the ten years since you informed me that your life was going in a whole new direction, my life has also taken some twists and turns, all because of a crazy cat lady with a baby who wouldn't stop crying. I was doing an emergency medicine rotation when another intern and I got caught up in the case of an infant who kept screaming in pain. Numerous workups in multiple facilities by a host of doctors couldn't figure out why. Everyone assumed it was colic and psychologic tension, because the mother was such an uptight nut job. Until we got a tip from an acupuncturist, no one suspected the real cause of her distress. She had something called ALCAPA syndrome. I'll let you look it up.

That baby is now eleven years old. Her mother sends me a picture of her and her nine siblings and their ten kitty-cats, every Christmas.

The other intern who got caught up in this case turned out to be the man I married, Brody Jones. We have a five-year-old daughter named Avery, a three-year-old son named Riley, an old Maine coon cat named Hairy Potter, and a rescued beagle named Hermione.

Brody finished his nine years of training as a pediatric heart surgeon last year. He did five years of general surgery residency, two years of cardiovascular surgery fellowship and another two years of fellowship in pediatric cardiology. He's now on staff at several major medical centers here in Salt Lake City.

After three years of my psychiatry residency, and with my husband still in training, I did another three years of internal medicine residency, and then, two years of acupuncture training. My interest in clinical medicine and having a family squelched my interest in research.

I now serve as the medical director of a refugee health center where we provide emergency and primary care. Because the predominant local church is always recruiting followers from around the world, many languages are spoken in Salt Lake City, and it's kind of an international hub. I get to use all of my foreign languages. It's also near great skiing, and Brody and I occasionally find time to take a few runs.

I hope everything has worked out well for you and that one of these days; we can catch up in person. Again, congratulations on your research.

Love always,

Dewy Meadows-Jones

Epilogue

In the course of her medical training in the early 1980s, author Beverly Hurwitz MD witnessed a case of ALCAPA, upon which this novel is based.

In that real-life case, the mother of a screaming infant was not only considered crazy by her care providers, but the professionals had almost succeeded in convincing this mother that she was crazy, and that it was her emotional instability that was making her baby so irritable.

However, an internal voice in that mother kept telling her that she was right, and that there was something terribly wrong with her infant daughter, and that the doctors just weren't smart enough to figure it out. So, she kept searching until she found that one doctor who knew. Unfortunately, that baby's ALCAPA did not get diagnosed until it was too late, and the infant died from heart failure before surgery could save her.

Of the tens of thousands of sick and injured people the author has attended to over the course of a multi-decade medical career, none ever impacted her as profoundly as the case of the screaming baby with the crazy mother who wasn't crazy.

Acknowledgments

I am enormously grateful for the help I received from Nancy Costo, whose astute observations and editing were instrumental to the creation of this story. I also appreciate the help I received from Ken Hurwitz, Jodyne Roseman, Amy Schapiro and Margie Hurwitz. Thanks are also extended to my publishing guru Katie Mullaly, and to my medical mentor, Dr. Richard Jaeger, who taught me to always assume that the patient is ill before assuming that he/she is crazy.

About the Author

Dr. Beverly Hurwitz, originally from Brooklyn, New York, has spent her professional life as a physician, educator, and author.

In her youth she won awards for scholastic journalism and served as copy editor for her college newspaper. Before attending medical school, she spent a decade as a health and physical education teacher in rural public schools.

As a medical fellow, Beverly specialized in the care of children with neurologic disability. After three decades of clinical practice, she spent eight years as a medical case analyst/writer for administrative law judges in federal and state court systems. In recent years, she has been writing novels and hiking books.

Beverly divides her personal time between reading, writing, golfing, hiking, skiing, and ice skating. She lives with her husband and rescued dachshunds in Utah.

Made in the USA
Middletown, DE
20 August 2022

70774535R00125